SECRET SIMON

A HAVEN HART NOVEL

DAVIDSON KING

Secret Simon

A Haven Hart Novel

Copyright © 2021 Davidson King

Website: https://www.davidsonking.com

ALL RIGHTS RESERVED

Cover design by: Designs by Morningstar

Editing done by: Flat Earth Editing & Proofreading

Proofreading provided by: Flat Earth Editing & Proofreading and Anita Ford

Interior Design and Formatting provided by: Flawless Touch Formatting

The unauthorized reproduction or distribution of this copyrighted work is illegal. No part of this book may be reproduced or transmitted in any form or by any means, including electronic or mechanical means, including photocopying, recording, or by any information storage and retrieval systems, without express written permission from the author, Davidson King. The only exception is in the case of brief quotations embodied in reviews.

This book is a work of fiction. While references may be made to actual places and events, the names, characters, places, and incidents either are products of the author's imagination or are used fictitiously. Any resemblance to actual persons, living or dead, events, or locales is entirely coincidental.

Licensed material is being used for illustrative purposes only and any person depicted in the licensed material is a model.

TRADEMARK

No part of this publication may be reproduced, stored in a retrieval system, or transmitted, in any form or in any means – by electronic, mechanical, photocopying, recording or otherwise – without prior written permission, except in the case of the brief quotations embodied in the critical reviews and certain other noncommercial uses permitted by copyright law. Please purchase only authorized electronic or print editions and do not participate in or encourage the electronic piracy of copyrighted material. Your support of the author's rights is appreciated. This book is a work of fiction. Names, characters, places, and incidents are a product of the author's imagination or are used fictitiously. Any resemblance to actual events, locales, or persons, living or dead, is coincidental. All products and/or brand names mentioned are registered trademarks of their respective holders/companies.

WARNING

This book contains violence and mention of suicide. Recommended for ages 18 years and up.

AUTHOR'S NOTE

I want to take a moment to mention an organization mentioned in this book. Trans Lifeline is and organization that provides support for the trans community. It is run by and for trans people. If you'd like to know more or to see how you can support this organization, the website is https://translifeline.org

Thank you for reading and I hope you enjoy. Be sure to read all the way to the end for some future news about my books.

I've come a long way since my first book, Snow Falling. I'm still not failing, Mrs. Raskin. So, I say again, fuck you.

PROLOGUE

My name is Simon, but you can call me Eight—I'll explain that later—and this is the story of how my hope for a quiet drama-free college life blew up in my face…all because I fell in love.

Yes, I know, cheesy. But here's the thing—it really is true. It's more complex than that, and it wouldn't be much of a story if it was all, "Met a boy, he was cool, we fell in love, the end."

Truth is, I chose to go to college five hours from Haven Hart, where I grew up, not because I had a bad childhood or hated my family, but because everyone knew who I was there…Hell, everyone knew who I was for miles and miles from there. If you don't know why, let me fill you in real fast.

I'm the nephew of the most powerful mob boss in Haven Hart, Christopher Manos. He isn't your typical mobster, though. I've seen the documentaries on Al Capone and Joe Bonanno, and yeah, sure, my uncle killed and isn't clean in a lot of ways. But he's also the best man I know. My mom died when I was a baby, and he loved me as a son and raised me as far away from his lifestyle as possible…Or at least, he tried to. No matter how hard he tried, though, there was no way to hide that kind of stuff forever.

As a child I saw a lot of things I shouldn't have, but when I was eight everything changed. There's that number again. See, I got bored waiting in a car while my pops's driver—Pops is what I call my uncle—went into the ice cream shop to get me some rocky road. So, I left the car and wandered around. That wasn't a good idea, and yet it kinda was.

A couple of guys started hassling me. One was named Roy Sokolov, and he tried to kidnap me. But from the depths of a dark, dank alley came my guardian angel. His name is Snow. He saved me that day, and we saved him too. He and my pops fell in love, and that's how I found the second-best person in my life. Snow, he calls me Eight—the age I was when he saved me—and because when he asked me what to call me, I wouldn't give him my name and only my age...I think you get the picture.

After that night, I saw so much more. Years later, my pops and I were actually kidnapped. There was no escaping the life he lived and so, when it came time to go to college, I decided it should be far away in the hopes that no one would know who I was.

Snow suggested I use a different last name, and while it hurt my heart to do it, I knew he was right. There were forgeries made, and *abracadabra*! I became Simon Mancia.

Thankfully, I got through my first year of college easily. No one knew who I was—at least no one said anything. I dated a few people. Penelope for about six months, but we didn't click the way a boyfriend and girlfriend should...Instead, she became my best friend. Then there was Raul. He was amazing, but he cheated on me after two months, and yeah...that sucked. I hadn't been with anyone since. That was, until I saw *Him*. He was singing karaoke on the green at campus when I returned my second year. It was some welcome-back thing, and he was right there and...*Wow*.

Penelope told me his name was Rush, and that was all she

knew. I decided it would be my mission to find out more and hope beyond hope that he'd take me up on an offer for coffee.

Well, there's something to be said for falling in love with someone; you will risk it all. I did just that and more.

So, sit back and find out how my finally calm life was turned upside down…all because I fell in love.

CHAPTER ONE

Simon

"You're late!" Penelope opened my driver's side door as soon as I put my car in park.

"How am I late? Classes don't start for three days." I had to squeeze between the door and my car since she was leaning on it.

"You said you'd be here by noon." She made a show of looking at her watch. "It's almost two, and we were supposed to go to the grocery store together."

I opened my trunk and started pulling out my suitcases and boxes. "And are grocery stores closed now?"

Penelope Rose was fierce and a little overbearing, but she was also my best friend.

"No, smartass, but by the time we get all your things to your room and unpacked it'll be dinnertime and we'll have lost our chance."

"You're dramatic, Penny." She hated when I called her that, but she sort of deserved it for greeting me with so much hostility.

"Fuck you, Simon!"

I chuckled as I closed the trunk. "Were you able to get a flatbed to help me get all this up to my dorm?"

With a roll of the eyes, she sashayed to the sidewalk where the flatbed was. "I did because *I* keep *my* promises."

"You don't get it, Pen, my dads are clingy. Leaving isn't easy, and even though they had me for a whole summer, it didn't matter. My stepdad, he still thinks I'm a kid sometimes and feels the need to tell me how the world is." I hauled the boxes onto the flatbed while Penelope held it in place so it didn't roll away.

"That's sweet, though. My folks waved when I left." Penelope didn't have the best family life. They didn't hurt her or anything; they were simply done with parenting, and when she turned eighteen, they'd started treating her more like a friend of the family. It was weird and complicated.

"Yeah, it is sweet, so stop hassling me." When the last of my things were on the flatbed, we walked toward the building.

"I don't get why they didn't just come up here with you since they had such a hard time letting you go. That way you might have made it on time."

They would have loved to bring me back to college for my second year like they did my first, but no one could know their identities, and while they'd been careful, it wasn't enjoyable to be rushed. Snow being forced to cover his white hair and Pops having to dodge people who were trying to see his face—not good. Going by the last name Mancia and not Manos kept me safe...and them. If I was going to be over five hours away from them, with no security, I had to protect myself somehow and not have anything slingshot back to them and risk their safety.

"It's a long drive, Pen, and while they do love me, they can't be away that long. It's cool, I'm here, and grocery stores are open late." I nudged her shoulder as she stepped into the building to hold the door for me.

We rode the elevator up to the fifth floor, where my room was.

I was lucky enough to get a single this year. I hated my roommate last year. He was messy, refused to shower, and had a new woman in his bed every night. When I told Snow about it, he'd patted my shoulder and said, "You're allowed to make a fussy over that hussy. I'm sure next year will be better." So, I wasn't surprised when a week later, my *single* room assignment arrived.

"Nice room." Penelope gawked as she stepped in. It *was* really nice. I had a corner room with three windows; one actually took up an entire corner, giving me great light and a view of the college green.

"I heard there was a last-minute dropout, and my dad snagged it up. He's always got his ear to the ground."

Penelope nodded as she tore open one of my boxes. I'd made sure anything that would identify me was tucked away in the duffle bag I had on my shoulder.

"Since you have this room to yourself, there is no rush to unpack sooooo—"

"You want to go to the store?"

She nodded and smiled brightly. "Fine." I went over to the window just to get a good look at everyone arriving, and I saw a stage set up. "What's going on there?"

Penelope came over and squinted. "Oh, yeah, it's a welcome-back karaoke thing the college is doing."

"Karaoke?" Snow loved karaoke and would often drag me to sing with him.

Penelope smirked at me. "Wanna go take a look before we go to the store?"

"Of course." I scoffed, dumped my duffle onto the bed, and quickly made for the door.

The campus was buzzing with excitement. Everyone was always happy to return after a long break and for most, this was a freedom they didn't get normally. Too often I heard stories about kids who were stuck working all summer to pay for their courses or their parents filling their free time with things to do when they got home. While I had responsibilities over the summer, Pops and Snow gave me my space too.

Abernathy University was everything I'd dreamed it would be. I knew I'd see it through the four years, and hopefully when I graduated I'd remember this place fondly.

As we got closer to the stage, I saw a lot of people surrounding it and listening to some girl belting out "Move You" by Kelly Clarkson. She was extraordinary, but she was no Kelly. Everyone was swaying and shouting in encouragement. She smiled and enthusiastically worked the crowd.

We listened to a few more people before deciding to run to the store to get what we needed. I drove since she didn't have a car, and we made fast work of getting everything. I had a meal plan with the university, but Snow and Pops made sure I never wanted for anything and always filled my account.

"You make me look like a monster," she said as she put her candy corn, chips, and soda on the belt.

"How?"

She gestured to my cart. "All healthy with your apples, and rice cereal. *Ugh*. Is that yogurt?"

I laughed and grabbed the divider so I could put my things on the belt too. "You're not a monster, I just eat this way is all."

"Mmhmm." She paid and waited for me while I was rung up.

When we returned to the university, the karaoke thing was still happening. My windows were rolled down, and I heard thunderous applause.

"What's going on there?"

Penelope looked and chuckled. "Clearly someone they all love."

I parked the car and got out. "I'm going to look, be right back."

I went over to the stage just as "Islands in the Stream" started playing, and I froze when the guy standing next to the woman from earlier started singing. He was the most beautiful man I'd ever seen. I recognized it was completely superficial of me, but I couldn't take my eyes off him. He was singing, smiling, dancing. His hair glinted off the rays of the sun. Brown and blond, all in one. Like caramel. And he was magnetic.

When the song ended, Penelope was by my side. "He's good, right?"

"Who is he?"

Just then another song began, and this time he was alone on the stage, and "Love You like a Love Song" by Selena Gomez started, and damned if he didn't hook me the second he opened his mouth.

I didn't feel myself getting closer to the stage, but suddenly I was right there at the edge. He wasn't facing me but instead was singing to the people on the other side, and *holy shit* I wanted his attention on me.

When he turned, my heart skipped a beat. He looked right at me and smiled. Fucking smiled and I was a goner. He danced my way, the whole time watching me like I was him. I hadn't noticed Penelope follow me over to the stage, but I heard her when she whispered into my ear.

"That's Rush."

For a minute I thought she'd said that was a rush, and I agreed but soon realized she was answering my earlier question.

"Rush, what?"

She shrugged. "Don't know. He's just always introduced as Rush."

"Introduced?" I found I needed to know so much about him.

"Yes, Romeo. He works at The Falsetto Café. The place I tried dragging you to a million times when we were dating last year but you always said no. He performs there. He's amazing."

I could have kicked myself for not going with her now, but no sense in dwelling on the past.

"I'm going to go talk to him."

She chuckled. "Good luck and be quick, you have food in your trunk."

I assumed she meant it as a friend would before talking to someone they were interested in, but as I approached him I realized she'd meant good luck even getting to him. People were surrounding him, begging for his attention.

I tried to break through the crowd several times only to be elbowed by some asshole, and when I thought I'd made my way through, Rush was gone.

"Hey." I turned toward Penelope.

"Where'd he go?"

"Probably far from all you insane people. Come on, let's put our food away. We can catch one of his shows at the café this week."

With a sigh, I agreed and followed her back to my car. I would make it a point to visit The Falsetto Café and meet this guy who I was sure would play a main role in my dreams tonight.

CHAPTER TWO

Rush

I walked fast, but not too fast, through the green to get to the bookstore to pick up my books. I'd known once I stepped foot on that stage I'd get sucked into the freeing feeling of entertaining, and my glutes were getting a workout as I raced to the store, but I didn't regret doing karaoke. A quick look at my watch told me I had ten minutes. I could do this.

"Hi, Rush."

I waved at the girl whose name I couldn't remember.

"Hiya, Rush!" An exuberant kid started walking next to me. "Great singing over there."

"Thank you." I smiled, trying not to make him feel like I didn't want to talk to him, but if I were late...*ugh*, it would be a pain.

"I heard you sing at the café down the street, yeah?"

I nodded. "I do. Friday and Saturday nights."

He started getting out of breath, and I knew he'd drop off. "Okay, well, see you there sometime."

"For sure," I said louder as I walked even faster, distancing myself from him.

I got to the counter at the bookstore and collapsed in a heap. I needed to work out more if rushing across campus knocked the wind out of me.

"You're almost late."

I looked up at Fred. He was a sweetheart to everyone but me. For some reason the guy didn't like me, and that was why I had to hurry to get here on time. If I didn't get my books at the scheduled time, he would tell my father and I would have to hear why I must set a better example.

"Almost isn't late, Fred."

"Semantics, Rush."

I rolled my eyes when he wasn't looking. "May I have my books, please?"

He turned on his heels and walked away. I hoped that meant he was going to get them. As I waited, I looked around the bookstore. There were so many photos in fancy frames on the walls, showing all the years of Abernathy University. The ones from many years ago were not as clear as the more recent ones. Some were sepia and some black and white. There was one that hung over the counter. A large man in a suit with suspenders, a handlebar mustache with a cigar hanging out of his mouth. A shovel, point down, digging into the dirt beside him. His smile was bright and obviously, judging by all the photos, an Abernathy trait. The small golden plaque below the picture read, *Abernathy University, Groundbreaking Ceremony: Harold Abernathy – 1840.*

"Here." Fred dropped the four books I needed on the counter, loudly.

"Thanks." I grabbed them and turned to leave, when he spoke again.

"I'm having dinner with your father tomorrow tonight. He wants some updates."

I did not need to face him to know there was a pretentious expression on his freckled face.

"Have fun with that," was all I said, and then I left the bookstore.

I shook off the residual frustration I always felt after an encounter with Fred and made my way over to Greta Hall, which was where private housing was, where I had my own dorm.

As I went up to my room, I received the usual hellos from anyone and everyone I encountered and by the time I shut the door, I was exhausted.

It was hard being held to such a high standard and because of that responsibility, I couldn't be an asshole. I always had to return smiles, could never shame my family's good name.

With a *thud*, I dropped my books on the desk and plopped onto the bed. I was scheduled to work at The Falsetto Café tomorrow, which meant tonight I was able to chill and forget everything. I planned on ordering pizza, catching up on my Netflix shows, and shutting the world out. And that was exactly what I did.

"Hey, Rush," the owner of the café, Luis, greeted me as I came in for my shift.

"Hi, Luis." I smiled at the man who, while in his late sixties, was still gorgeous.

He'd opened The Falsetto Café in the late '90s after his partner of over twenty years had passed away from AIDS. Luis once told me that in his partner's prime he'd had the most amazing voice, and they'd fallen in love through music, and after he was alone it was music that had saved him. So, he'd decided to take that and open this café.

"Are you ready to sing, my little bird?" He handed me a cup of herbal tea, the kind I drank to soothe my throat right before performing.

"Yes. I've got some good ones for you tonight." I shot him a wink and moved to the back, where there was a small dressing room.

A lot of students and faculty came into the café often; it was how so many people knew me. Not because of my father or my family, but because of my talent, and that was something that was all mine. No one could take it from me.

The Falsetto Café construct was perfect—the design was unique, and there wasn't an ounce of the place where you didn't feel the love Luis had for it.

A stage was set up, naturally, and there were small tables filling the floor. If you looked up at the ceiling, there were musical scales hanging with notes that gleamed. The long bar that ran along the side of the café had a piano countertop. It didn't make noise, but it lit up whenever you touched the keys. Behind the bar was a huge mirror, and etched in the glass was a perfect silhouette of Freddie Mercury when he'd performed with his band Queen at the Live Aid concert in 1985. Luis said he and his partner, Jim, were able to see it in person and it was otherworldly.

I had just finished putting on a touch of foundation—I was not a fan of wearing makeup, but it helped to keep my face from looking shiny under the hot lights—when Luis came in to tell me I could hit the stage as soon as I was ready.

It was a full house, which was no shock since this was such a popular place. I took to the stage, microphone in hand, and smiled at all the faces.

"Good evening, everyone, it's so great to be here tonight as usual." That garnered a few laughs. "I have some good songs for everyone, and Luis also told me to let you know that the Saturday after next is the open mic charity night. All proceeds from cover charges to payments for drinks and food will go to The Jim Bastian Memorial Fund. It's a charity that helps people who are diagnosed with HIV or AIDS get financial help for medical payments and medication. Wonderful charity, so I hope to see each and every one of you here then."

I scanned the crowd. I was unable to see many of them due to the lights on my face, but it made them feel as if I were giving each of them a little of my attention.

Placing the microphone into the stand next to the piano, I took my seat and let my fingers play some Elton John. The cheers began immediately, and I got lost in my music.

Song after song was met with thunderous applause, and the audience joined in when they knew the lyrics. I performed for a straight hour before thanking them and announcing that I needed a break.

Over at the bar, Luis had a glass of water waiting and a smile. "You're so talented, Rush. I don't know why you don't reach for the stars and do this when you graduate."

"What, play here forever?" The water was cool and soothed my tired throat.

"I wish, but no. Come on, you're talented. You should be on stages all over the world, making the boys drop their briefs for you."

I chuckled and placed the glass on the bar top. "As wonderful as that sounds, you know my father would never be okay with that."

Luis sighed as he often did when we talked about my father and the future he had in store for me.

"That man needs to realize you're old enough to make your own choices and—"

"Luis, I know. It's more complicated than that."

"Mmhmm, it always is." He was quiet for a moment, and I realized he was looking at something at the end of the bar. When I turned, I saw a guy, his dark hair and even darker eyes immediately noticeable. He had on black-rimmed glasses, and damned if he was not striking. "He's been staring at you."

Scoffing I turned to Luis. "Probably loved the set I did."

"Yeah, I see how all people watch you and that man over there...he likes your ass-sets."

I playfully pushed Luis. "Shut it."

Luis let it go and walked the tables to see how all the patrons were doing before I did my next set. I sat there sipping my water, but in the corner of my eye the beautiful man was still there, and I knew from the way the hairs stood on the back of my neck that he was staring at me. I figured I'd see if he was interested in me the way Luis assumed. I faced his direction, met his gaze, and tipped my drink at him.

Of course, what happened after that could only be described as a disaster...for him. He lifted his hand to wave and in doing so knocked his drink—which was full—over. It splashed the woman beside him, who turned to see what happened, and she knocked her drink onto the floor, which startled the gentleman behind her, and the guy who I found to be quite beautiful was apologizing profusely, offering to buy everyone drinks.

It took everything in me to not laugh and since I felt terrible, I thought I'd go over and help. When I got over there, it was still chaos.

"These are brand new shoes!" the woman yelled.

"But I didn't get my drink on your shoes; your drink is on your shoes because you dropped your glass," Cutie said to her.

"Which I wouldn't have done had you not poured yours on me."

"I didn't pour—"

"Hey," I interrupted, "how about we calm down and all get

fresh drinks?" I glanced at the woman's shoes, which were far from ruined. "Nothing a little seltzer can't fix."

She opened and closed her mouth a few times before releasing a breath. "Yeah, okay, fine."

I smiled at Cutie, who was looking at me while tossing money on the counter. "You can get whatever you'd like," he said as sweet as could be.

The woman grunted and took the bills without even a thank-you. I gave Cutie my attention and grinned. "How about I buy you a drink?"

He was frozen for a moment, and then like the sun coming out after a storm, he smiled, and it was like sunshine after the rain.

CHAPTER THREE

Simon

I'm not a clumsy person, never have been. Yet there I was, in front of the most gorgeous guy I had ever seen, causing havoc and spilling things everywhere. He was probably offering to buy me a drink out of sympathy, but fuck it, I would take it.

"What were you drinking?" He gestured for us to move away from the irate woman who didn't seem to understand what an apology meant.

"I was just drinking a soda actually. I only turned twenty recently." I knew twenty was old for a sophomore, but due to a crazy psychopath kidnapping Pops and me, I ended up having to make up the school year when I suffered some mental setbacks. No one made mention of my age, I figured most didn't give a shit.

He nodded and ordered soda for me and water for himself. "You go to Abernathy?"

"I do, this is my second year."

His brows rose. "And I've never seen you before?"

Chuckling I answered, "It's a big campus, you can't see everyone."

He shrugged and took the drinks the bartender gave us. We walked over to a table next to the stage that had a reserved placemark on it, which I assumed was for him.

"I just think I'd see you a mile away." I was glad I wasn't drinking at that moment because I totally would have choked.

"That's nice. Funny you mention that. I saw you yesterday on the green. You were phenomenal, and my friend told me you performed here. Figured, since classes didn't start yet, I'd come check you out."

He smiled as he sipped his water. "I'm glad you did."

I wanted to talk more, but he looked over to the stage and stood up. "I have to do my next set, but sit and enjoy your soda, and maybe…if you want, when I'm done, we can talk some more."

"I'd like that."

I sat there through his entire next set, drinking my soda and getting pulled in by his magnetic presence. The crowd adored him, and it was easy to see why. You felt, even though he was performing for everyone, he was singing just for you.

When his set was over, he jumped off the stage and asked me to wait for him while he changed. And then he disappeared backstage, and I waited.

———

"I never got your name," he said to me as we were walking to campus from the café. It was a perfect night, not too cold and not too hot.

"Simon."

"I'm Rush."

"Yeah, I knew that."

He nodded. "So, what's your major, or are you undecided?"

This was always complicated, but I had come to master the

ability to maneuver around questions about my family. "I'm actually majoring in business."

"That's smart. Want to open your own company or something?"

I shook my head. "Nah, not at all, but my pops has a business, and I'll likely take over for him. What about you, what's your major?"

Always push the conversation back to talking about others when you don't want to delve into your family too much. That was something Bill had taught me. Bill worked for my pops, and while it hadn't started out easy for him, he'd become vital to the security of our family.

"Seems you and I are both looking to follow into our fathers' footsteps, but while you're aiming for business, I'm majoring in English."

I couldn't have hidden the shock in my voice if I'd tried. "You're not majoring in theater or the arts of some sort?"

His laugh was haunting, and my heart panged for whatever loss he was feeling. "No, that's not the family way."

"But you're how old? Aren't you allowed to choose for yourself what you want to do for the rest of your life?"

He stopped walking and faced me. "I could say the same thing about you."

"But you assume I don't want to take over for my pops. I can tell you'd rather do anything but step into your father's shoes."

Rush scoffed. "You just met me, and already you think you know me so well?"

"I know people. I read them *very* well—another family thing. I can see you'd rather be singing on a stage than...whatever it is your father does."

"I would love to entertain people, but it's complicated," he argued. *Complicated, ha!* I knew complicated better than anyone.

"You'd be surprised how well I understand the complex weavings of family dilemmas, Rush. More than you can even know, believe me. But I also know that if I told my pops I didn't want to do it, he'd say okay because he loves me."

Rush's eyes widened. "So, now you're saying not only am I letting my father pull my strings, but he also doesn't love me?"

"I didn't say that." This was turning into a disaster.

"You implied it, though."

I released a sigh. "I'm sorry. I don't know your life, and we did just meet. I have no right telling you what you should or shouldn't do with your future."

Rush stared at me, and for a moment, the sounds of people walking around us were muffled. "Follow me for a second," he said, and then he was off, speed-walking, almost.

"Wait, where are we going?"

"I want to show you something. Keep up, slowpoke."

We walked for a good five minutes, stopping at the statue garden. That was what I called it, at least. It was ten statues of men in a semicircle, a triangular sculpture in the center with names covering it.

"Why are we here?"

Rush walked over to the first statue. "This is Lawrence Abernathy. He designed the grounds here at the university." He moved to the next. "Meet Theodore Abernathy. He was what you'd call the CEO of the university for a time." One after another, Rush named all the people until he got to the last two. "This one here is Rushmore Abernathy the First; this one is Rushmore Abernathy the Second, and I"—he held his arms wide open—"am Rushmore Abernathy the Third."

Well, shit.

"Like I said, it's complicated, Simon. All these people, every one, was an Abernathy. This institution is built by us and must stand because of us. I was born into this obligation."

"I get it."

He took a few steps toward me, stopping a couple of inches from my face. "Do you, though?"

"Yeah."

"How?"

"I just do. I mean, my family built their own empire, so to speak, but no one ever expected me to be part of it; I want to be."

He stepped away, a small smile on his face. "This got too deep, don't you think?"

"For sure." I grinned. "Maybe we stick to simpler questions like what's your favorite color, or best action movie, things like that."

Rush tapped his chin. "Red and *Twister*."

I chuckled. "Red and *Twister*, okay, I can work with that. I like the color blue, and my favorite action movie would probably have to be *Avengers*, the first one." We started walking again, back toward the dorms.

"Oh, now hold on, you said action movie, not favorite superhero movie."

"I didn't say it couldn't be a superhero movie, though."

He scoffed and rolled his eyes. "That's totally unfair. I was thinking outside all the obvious superhero action ones."

I just shrugged. "Don't know what to tell ya, Rush. You gotta think on a broader scale."

His laugh was husky, and I was really glad the heavy conversation was over. I wanted to get to know this guy, not scare him away or make him feel uncomfortable.

"What dorm are you in?" he asked.

"Roosevelt Hall, you?"

"Greta."

We reached the part of campus where the paths split toward the individual dorms. Greta was to the right and my dorm to the left.

"I did enjoy talking to you," Rush said.

"I'd like to do more talking if you're interested, and I promise to keep the conversation light."

He smiled and grazed his hand over my arm. "I'd like that."

"Great, gimme your cell and I'll put my number in, and you can text me so I have yours. And maybe, if you're up to it, this weekend after we find out all the crap our professors are thrusting on us, we can catch a movie or dinner?"

He smiled and handed me his phone. "Perfect."

I put my number in and handed it back to him. I was relieved when he texted me while I was right there.

"See you soon, Simon." He slipped his phone into his pocket.

"Yeah, same."

I watched as he walked down the path toward Greta Hall. He didn't look over his shoulder once, and I tried not to read into that too much. When I could no longer see him, I took my own path to my dorm, thinking about that smile and amazing voice.

CHAPTER FOUR

Rush

I was having a wonderfully delicious dream about a certain dark-eyed guy on his knees, choking on my dick, when a blaring noise had me bolting straight up on my bed. The phone my father had installed in my room because, in his words, "I know you put your cell phone on silent, and I must be able to reach you when I need you." Yeah, it was ringing.

"Hello?" I cleared the sleep out of my voice the best I could, but it was no use, he heard.

"Are you still sleeping, Rushmore? It's nearly eleven."

"I don't have class until tomorrow, and I was enjoying being lazy for a whopping twenty-four hours, Father."

"Sarcasm is an ugly trait, Rushmore."

I rolled my eyes, glad he couldn't see me since he'd surely have something to say about it. "Is there something you need?"

"As a matter of fact, there is. I'd like you to come to my office on campus at noon sharp. That leaves you seventy minutes to arrive."

I turned my head to see the clock on my alarm. Sure enough, my father was exactly right. "Is this something we could maybe talk about on the phone?"

His sigh was loud. "You know I prefer looking at people when I speak to them, something you should want as well. Expressions can be hidden over the phone, but face-to-face, all is revealed."

Ridiculous. "Okay, see you then."

"Don't be late," he said, and there was a loud click.

I placed the phone back on the receiver and slowly got out of bed. Meetings with my father were never catch-ups on how life was. They were filled with lectures and things I needed to be doing.

I knew I had to look my best; even though my father would have something to say about my appearance, I wanted to limit the criticism. I grabbed my Ralph Lauren designer chinos, a light-blue button-down collar-piqué shirt, and my tan Vans. Got the usual briefs and socks, and my shower caddy, and went to wash up.

My wardrobe was separated into clothes I liked to wear and the ones my father expected me to be seen in. This ensemble was all for good old Dad. I made quick work of washing, brushing my teeth and hair, and getting dressed. My father's office was on the other side of campus, and it would probably take me twenty minutes to get over there.

As I meandered across campus people said hello, some walking a bit with me, telling me how they'd enjoyed my show the night before. A few were wondering what classes I had. By the time I got to Washington Hall, where my father's office was, I had easily spoken with ten people.

I climbed the stairs to the third floor and walked right up to Holly, my father's receptionist.

"Hey, Rush, you ready for classes?"

Holly was a sunny person. I honestly didn't know how she worked for my father or what she did for him. She was in her thirties, I suspected, with golden-blonde curly hair, cornflower eyes, always had on bright red lipstick, and her smile was welcoming.

"I am, but I'll miss sleeping in."

We both chuckled but abruptly stopped when the door to my father's office opened.

"Rushmore, don't dillydally, come in."

Holly mouthed she was sorry, though for what, I didn't know. I simply shrugged and made my way over to the office.

My father was already back behind his desk when I walked in. I shut the door and sat across from him...waiting.

He wanted me to be on time but there he was, shuffling through papers, not saying a word, making *me* wait. Finally, he set his papers on the desk and looked at me as if I were a student in trouble.

"I had dinner with Frederick last night." *Oh, fucking hell.*

"Okay?"

"He told me you were singing at the karaoke affair on the green."

"I was."

He nodded. "He told me you made quite a spectacle up there, and then barely made it to the bookstore for your scheduled pickup."

Narrowing my eyes, I leaned forward slightly. "Is Fred some spy for you or something, and is there a reason you feel the need to have me watched?"

"Rushmore, relax. He and I merely conversed over dinner. You came up and, well, the rest is history, as you say."

"I don't say that. The idiom is, 'The rest is history.' John Wade coined it in 1839. But the issue with that, Father, is the phrase tends to imply that the story is known and therefore history everyone is privy to. Unfortunately, I haven't the faintest idea what you're talking about. Fred spies, he's an asshole to me, and he longs to get you to frown upon everything I do." I chuckled darkly. "Little does he realize you already do."

My rant was out of character for me, and the openmouthed, wide-eyed expression on my father's face proved that.

"Rushmore, what's gotten into you? You sass me, you sleep late, you're acting out—"

"Acting out, how? This here? No, this is me saying I've had enough. I'm twenty-one, and I don't need you fathering me like some toddler. I am majoring in what you want me to major in, and if I want to do karaoke or work at the café in my spare time, that's what I'll do. Tell Fred if he continues to harass me, I'll file a complaint against him."

"I have no idea what's come over you, Rushmore, but I don't like it."

"Nothing has, I don't like being called in here for you to critique my every step. I'm tired of it. I have the best GPA you could possibly get, everyone on campus likes me, except Fred, and for the most part, I'm happy. What I need is for you to let me be a grown-up, or I'll transfer out of this university so fast, you'll wish you had more children than just me to keep your legacy at Abernathy University alive."

I was done. I'd left my father speechless, so without another word, I walked out of his office and toward my dorm as fast as my legs could take me. I was sure I hadn't heard the last of this, but for a moment, however brief, I was going to enjoy the freedom I'd unleashed in that office.

Four hours later, there was still no call from my father reaming me out for my outburst earlier in the day. I knew I wasn't going to be lucky enough to get zero blowback from it, but I would enjoy the silence for as long as I could.

With classes beginning the following day, I took out all my syllabi and made sure I had everything I needed. That didn't take long and I was insanely bored. I didn't know why I found myself in front of Roosevelt Hall, but I did. I looked up at the old building and wondered if Simon's room faced this way. Then I worried it did and that he would see me staring at him like some insane stalker.

To my right I saw a bench under a large tree, and I went over and sat down. What was I doing? We'd agreed that after classes started, we'd do something. *So why are you here, Rush? Don't suffocate a guy, what's the matter with—*

"Rush?"

That did not sound like my inner voice.

"Rush?" Simon sat beside me on the bench. "You okay?"

"Huh? Of course, why?" I tried to play it cool, but I was probably blowing it.

"I said your name a couple of times, but you were zoned out."

I took a second to run my gaze over him. He dressed really nice. Designer but casual without the haughtiness my father tended to like. He clearly came from money. His thick, dark hair was styled, and he had his glasses on, which I hadn't realized was a kink of mine until now.

"I was just taking a walk and sat down to take a break for a moment." Sure, that sounded believable.

He nodded. "Oh, are you headed somewhere?"

"No, probably just back to my dorm."

He had a sexy smirk. "Well, I was going to meet my friend Penelope at the cafeteria for dinner, wanna come?"

I was never so happy to have grabbed my wallet before leaving my dorm. I had my student ID in there, and that meant dinner with Simon…and whoever Penelope was.

"Yes, I could eat."

We smiled, and the shitty feeling over my craptastic day started to dissipate.

CHAPTER FIVE

Simon

Finding Rush on the bench outside of my building was sort of crazy, seeing as I'd been thinking about him while I got ready to go to dinner. Snow had called me last night, and being the perceptive person he is, he'd known I was hiding something. I didn't want to tell anyone about Rush yet, though, because I didn't know if it was going anywhere. Luckily he let it go, and we talked about classes and how things were going at home.

Pops had taken up a new hobby of clay shooting with Bill, which Snow said made for some boring conversations, and he'd threatened them both with bodily harm if they brought up the stupid sport while Snow was in the room. He'd tried all summer to get me to go with him, but I'd wanted nothing to do with it.

I chuckled, and that familiar pain of homesickness twisted in my heart, but I was glad to miss home. That meant it was a great place, and knowing I had amazing people in my life was enough to make me fulfill my dreams.

Rush and I bullshitted as we walked to the cafeteria, and I asked him how his day was.

"I had to meet with my father, hence this outfit, which I apologize to your eyes for having to see."

I didn't give a shit about what people wore.

"What's wrong with what you're wearing?"

Rush sighed and I thought he'd say more, but he clammed up.

Penelope was waiting outside the cafeteria when we got there and smiled as soon as she saw us.

"Oh, hey, are we dining for three this evening?" she joked.

"I hope that's all right." Rush appeared apprehensive now that we were here.

"She's messing with you, it's fine."

We went in, got our trays, and stood in line. I did have to say that Abernathy University had outstanding food. I'd heard horror stories from some of my friends about the food their colleges served and was relieved I didn't share their pain.

We sat close to the window and as soon as we started to eat, Penelope began her questions. "So, Rush, I've seen you play at The Falsetto Café and on the green the other day. You have one hell of a voice and stage presence; are you an art major?"

"English, actually."

"Really?" Her brow scrunched up. "Is it to help you with your performing?"

"No, I have no intention of performing for a living."

Penelope opened her mouth to say something else, but I decided to save the poor man. "Do you have a lot of classes this year?" It was a stupid question, but it was all I could think of off the top of my head.

"Yeah, but I've been able to space them well so I'm not racing all over campus."

The whole dinner felt disjointed. I wasn't sure if it was because Penelope was there or maybe it was a fluke the other night, and I'd simply *thought* Rush and I had connected when in fact we hadn't.

I found myself no longer hungry. Penelope and Rush were going on about some professor I wasn't familiar with, and I let my gaze sweep over the cafeteria. Everyone was out, shaking off the last of their absolute freedom before all their professors dragged them down with papers and projects. It wasn't overly loud, but oftentimes I could hear someone burst into laughter.

As I turned my gaze over to Rush again, I locked eyes with some guy who was literally glaring at our table. At least I thought it was our table. He seemed familiar, and I was trying to remember where I had seen him, when Rush called my name.

"Sorry, what? I was lost in my head."

Rush smiled. "It's okay, there's so much going on, and there's that nervous energy of wondering what horrors our professors will bestow upon us," he joked.

"Right?"

"Anyway, Penelope just told me that the two of you dated for a while."

Shit, why'd she do that? I looked over at her and she shrugged. "What, is it some super secret?"

"No, I don't know how that came up, though."

"Well, maybe if you weren't zoned out, you'd have heard," Penelope argued.

"I'm starting to see why the relationship didn't work," Rush joked.

"We're better as friends." Penelope shrugged and took the last bite of her burger.

I had just stood after we finished eating, and Rush asked me one of the questions I hated the most. "So, where do you live, Simon?"

"Roosevelt Hall, you know that already." I knew that wasn't what Rush meant, but it was so complicated.

"Funny guy, I meant when you're not at the university. Where's home?"

It was Penelope who laughed and answered the question. "Good luck trying to pry info out of Simon. He tells you just enough about himself to get by. Yet, another reason I couldn't be his girlfriend. Isn't that right, Secret Simon?"

"You make it sound like I'm in Witness Protection, Pen."

Rush's eyes widened. "Oh my God, are you?"

"No," I snorted. "I live five hours from here."

"Mmhmm, and that's so helpful." Penelope grabbed her tray and walked off.

"You have your reasons for secrecy, Simon. You don't have to tell anyone anything you don't want to." He patted my arm and walked away with his own tray.

The three of us spent a few hours meandering around campus, talking about our courses and Penelope going on and on about her whole life. She hid nothing, and I hid everything. When Penelope exclaimed she had to go to bed early for a seven o'clock class, Rush and I found ourselves blissfully alone.

"She's talkative," Rush said.

"That she is, but there's never that awkward silence with her. I like that."

"When's your first class tomorrow?"

"Not until nine." I tried hard not to have classes too early. I preferred later ones—I wasn't a morning person.

"Same for me." Rush turned and faced me, slightly shorter but only by maybe an inch. "Want to come to my dorm?"

I was unable to rein in my smile. "Sure."

As Rush and I walked across campus toward Greta Hall, I couldn't brush off the feeling that I was being watched. The closer we got to his dorm, the worse it felt, and by the time we were at the entrance, the hairs on the back of my neck were standing straight up.

"You okay?" he asked, obviously because I kept looking behind us the whole way.

"I'm fine, just…I keep feeling like someone is following us."

Rush's smile dropped, and he looked out along the campus green. "There are a lot of people out tonight, but I hate when I get that feeling."

Thing was, whenever I did get that feeling, I was always right, but I wasn't about to tell Rush that since then I would have to explain myself.

"Yeah, probably just first-day jitters or whatever. Come on."

"Maybe." I followed Rush inside and noticed how nice the building was. It was newer than mine, and more opulent, but when the university had your name on it, you probably got the best accommodations. Being the nephew of Christopher Manos, I understood how a name gave you power; I also knew how a name could destroy you.

When Rush opened the door to his room, I saw that he too had a single, but it didn't surprise me. "Nice."

"You didn't think my father would allow someone to share a room with me, did you?" he joked.

"Oh no, of course not." I played along.

He walked over to a mini fridge and took out two sodas. "Have a seat and a drink."

I took the soda and sat on the small love seat he had. "I have a single too but no love seat. I gotta get me one of these."

"It's nice, especially when you have someone in here who wants to talk, and you don't want them on your bed."

I bit my lip, loving how his gaze went to my mouth. "So, you don't want me on your bed?"

"Oh, I dunno, I very much hope to get you there eventually."

Fuck. There was no way I was standing up any time soon—my cock was like steel.

"Are you just gonna stand there, or maybe you want to sit with me on this too-small couch."

Rush chuckled but did come over. "You're trouble, Simon."

"Nah, not too much."

The second he sat beside me I felt his heat, and it was as if it drove right through me. I wanted to taste this man, feel him, wrap myself completely around him and not untangle until morning. But no, he wasn't a one-nighter. He felt like more, and I was so glad that the awkwardness from the cafeteria was long gone.

"Your eyes are like onyx," Rush said, his breath washing across my overheated face.

"I get that from my pops."

"I like it."

He was so fucking close I wanted to—"Can I kiss you?" I asked.

"If you don't, I'm sure as shit gonna kiss you, Simon."

I smiled into that kiss with Rushmore Abernathy the Third. And damn, the second his lips touched mine, it felt like an electric shock. Cheesy, I know, but it was like being plugged into a person and feeling and tasting them as if they were the best energy.

His tongue dipped into my mouth and I hummed. I swear I'd have sung if I could; he tasted like perfection. I grazed my tongue over his, and then he was pinning me to the love seat and attacking my mouth.

Nips from his teeth drove me wild, and I wrapped my legs around him, begging him closer.

"Fuck," Rush groaned into my mouth.

"I want you."

"We…" Kiss. "Need to…" I bit his lip… "Shit, we have to stop." He pushed off me so fast I still had my eyes closed and he was across the room.

"Why'd you stop?"

He was running his fingers through his hair, staring out the window. "If we keep going, I'll fuck you, Simon."

"I wouldn't complain." I released a breathy laugh.

He turned around and I could see how hard he was. "I don't

want to just fuck you. I like you. It's weird, right? We just met, but I know that I like being with you, and I want to keep doing this."

"I've thought all the same things."

"Simon, I don't want to sound like some old-fashioned guy, but…fuck it. I want to go slow with you. Not too slow." He cleared that up quickly. "But I want that date with you this weekend. I want to know about you and commiserate with you on things no one else understands but us. I get people who want to sleep with me because of who my father is, and they think it will do something amazing for them if they say they're my boyfriend. I don't get that feeling from you, like you want more than just me."

I stood and walked over to him. "I don't think I could handle more than just you, Rush."

"You don't want to run out of here screaming and telling everyone I'm some tease or whatever?"

I furrowed my brow. "I'm not like that. I don't talk about people's business, and I sure as shit don't talk about mine with anyone."

"I'd like to unravel some of your business, Secret Simon."

I smiled, hiding how terrifying that thought was. "We go slow, then."

"Yeah."

I pressed a quick kiss to his lips. "I need to get the fuck out of here before I jump you."

He laughed, but I was serious. "Okay."

"Have a good first day of class, Rush."

"You too, Simon."

CHAPTER SIX

Rush

Thank God for my alarm. I'd had sex dream after sex dream last night, and I was exhausted. As I trudged down the hallway to the showers, I knew I would have to hit the coffee cart on the way to my first class.

After I was showered and dressed, I grabbed my bag and headed out. It was sunny and there was a slight breeze, which was nice. I hated when it was humid and hot out because by the time I'd get across campus, my clothes would be drenched.

I got coffee at the cart and chugged it all the way to my creative nonfiction class. As I raced along the pathways, people waved, said hello, the typical. I did my best to respond to each and every person but if I stopped I'd be late, and I did not want that shit storm. These professors reported to my father and after my blowup yesterday, I knew he was itching to throw something in my face.

I arrived at Dickens Hall with ten minutes to spare, tossed my empty cup into the trash, and went to Professor McKinley's room.

When I opened the door I saw that it was almost full, but there were a few empty desks in the front of the room. I despised sitting in the front, but I wasn't going to have a choice in the matter, so I made my way over.

"Good morning, everyone, and welcome to Creative Nonfiction. My name is Professor McKinley, and I want to assure each and every one of you that this isn't an easy slide class. Many of you likely signed up for it to get some simple credits. Well, I assure you that if you did that, you might want to drop this class."

Professor McKinley was in her fifties. She was tough as nails and looked it too: Her blonde-and-silver hair was pulled back into a severe bun; she wore a long black skirt and a gray fitted shirt. Her glasses were the final touch in her angry-professor appearance.

I opened my laptop, took out the syllabus, and waited for her to start the lesson. Every professor today would be giving this same speech. Truth was, some of these classes *were* slide classes, but every professor seemed to get some sick joy in terrifying us. I knew this institution and the education system better than most, and Professor Regina McKinley did not instill fear in me.

She moved toward the board and caught my eye. "Good to see you, Rushmore." I gave her a quick nod, hoping that would be all she would say. This was the main reason I hated being in the front. The professors talked to me, and the class often assumed I was some favorite.

Thankfully she went to her smartboard and left me alone. I did a good job of not letting people know who I was. It was what had made telling Simon my story on the first day I met him...*Shit*. I could not go thinking about him or I would get hard.

I was in classes for the next few hours until a break at noon, and I was starving. I had a while until my last class of the day, so I decided to get a bite at the cafeteria.

I'd just scanned my card when Fred stood in front of me.

"Having a good first day, Rushmore?"

I rolled my eyes and walked around him. Either my father had never given Fred the message to leave me be or Fred was a masochist.

"That's rude, I was being nice." I grabbed a tray and moved toward the salads, ignoring Fred but making sure to say hello to anyone else who said hi. Was it childish? Yep. Did I care? Nope.

"Are you really going to ignore me?" Fred's voice rose, and a few people glanced our way.

"Leave me alone, Fred. Did dear old Dad not give you the message?" I grabbed a water and made my way to the sitting area.

"He did. He was quite cross with me, actually, and I was wondering if—"

I spun around so fast he almost crashed into my tray. "Fred, you've made it your job to make my life miserable for almost three years; do not even think about asking me for a damn thing. If you and my father had a falling out, that's on you. Now fuck off, or I will file a complaint against you for harassment."

Fred looked around nervously; more people were paying attention now, and I hoped they didn't hear too much of what I had to say. I believed the reason Fred hadn't blabbed who I was to everyone had something to do with the fact that he liked knowing something so few did.

"Fine," he whispered and speed-walked his way out of the cafeteria.

With everyone staring at me I didn't feel like sitting in there, so I took my salad and water, placed the tray back on the counter, and figured I'd go eat outside on one of the benches.

"Hey, you're Rush, right? Of course you are. I'm Emmanuel, but everyone calls me Em, please call me Em because I hate the name Emmanuel. It was my grandfather's, and he was not a nice man, if you get what I mean. Anyway, like I said, I'm Em, you're Rush. Right, so I have this thing I'm doing, here." This nonstop talking Em tossed a flyer at me, and luckily I grabbed it before the wind took it away.

"It's a charity thing I'm doing here on campus for transgender rights. And it's a talent show sort of thing, but more open mic. It's about people expressing themselves from the inside out, since we really...totally should see people for who they are, and that means getting to know and see them."

"Okay..."

"Right, maybe I should tell you more. So each person who enters is to do an act, or show their art, or like I said, whatever helps express themselves for who they are, also like auction something off. For example, my friend, Loli, she's a dancer, and she's going to do a dance for everyone to show what she can do, and then she's offering dancing lessons for an entire month, and people will bid. Another friend, Darnell, he's an amazing painter, and he's going to show off some of his work and offer three paintings, and people will bid for them. All proceeds are going to Trans Lifeline. It's a non-profit organization that offers emotional and financial support to trans people in crisis. For trans people by trans people."

"Wow, Em, this is insanely cool, but if it's for trans people by trans people, I'm not qualified."

Em seemed very jittery, but he smiled and gave me all his attention. I could see how much this meant to him.

"No, no, anyone can donate. It would be silly if the organization turned down money. I want to have this auction-charity-whatever-you-want-to-call-it and donate it to them."

"I'm not sure what I could offer to auction, though, Em."

He laughed, and it was one of those full-body laughs that was contagious and suddenly I was laughing too.

"Silly, Rush. You could offer someone a night at The Falsetto Café, maybe? Music lessons, anything."

I hadn't thought of that. "Okay, sure. When is it?"

He tapped the flyer. "Not until the week before winter break. I understand people need time to prepare. And I love the idea of donating to Trans Lifeline during the holidays."

I nodded. "Okay, thanks." I looked at the flyer. "This is your number?"

"Yes, and email."

"Wonderful. I'll contact you as soon as I can think of what I'll be auctioning off."

"Yes!" Em jumped up and was clapping with insane exuberance. "This will be amazing. I gotta run, bye." And then he was racing across the green.

Damn, that guy had a lot of energy. I read over the entire flyer and found myself getting excited about the prospect of doing this. After I graduated I'd likely be stuck at this university and would not get to live my passion of entertaining, so I wanted to grasp every opportunity I could now.

Of course, the first person I wanted to tell was Simon. I checked out the time and had twenty minutes until my next class. I shot him a text that I wanted to tell him something and what time I'd be free if he wanted to talk.

I tossed the rest of my lunch into the garbage, grabbed my bag, and walked toward my next class.

CHAPTER SEVEN

Simon

"It's a nightmare, Eight. I went over there, and the walls were yellow and not the happy sunshine yellow, I'm talking urine yellow." I grimaced at Snow's description of the new veterinarian's office for the dogs.

My childhood dog, Buck, had died a couple of years ago, but he'd left behind a bunch of offspring after impregnating a neighbor's French poodle. Snow had been determined to find homes for the Germadoodles, as he called them, but he fell in love with three of them, and so he had three large dogs, and I swore the old veterinarian retired because of those dogs.

"Thank God you're not hiring him for interior design then, huh?" I chuckled when he scoffed, and I threw my laptop in my bag.

"You're being sassy—that's my job. Now, tell me, how are classes?"

I rolled my eyes at his ridiculous question. "You do know this is the first day, and I've only gone to two classes and really can't make a judgment call on that."

"Yeah, but first impressions, Eight, what do you think?"

"They were fine."

The silence on the other end should have simply made me feel like I rendered Snow speechless, but no, this was not good. Silence meant he was winding up for—

"Eight, have I taught you nothing? You can tell a lot about a person by observing them. If they give a snide expression to a girl who has blonde hair and a smile to a brunette, it shows you they have preferences, and those blondes better be fucking rocket scientists."

"Snow, come on, I—"

"If you notice a professor looking at you kindly, use that. It could be a huge advantage."

"I'm there to learn, you know…gain knowledge, not get in with the personal side of their lives."

Snow huffed…*Well, shit.* "Eight! While knowledge is power, action is change. You might fail something and your personality, or how you act, could be the curve you need."

"Why are you assuming I'll fail?"

"I'm not. Shut up and don't try to make me feel guilty; it's genuinely impossible."

I felt a vibration against my cheek, looked at my screen, and saw a text from Rush.

"Snow, I gotta go, I have a text and I need to…I'll call you back after class."

"Who are they?"

"Huh?" Playing dumb with him was, well, dumb.

"Stupid is an ugly color on you. Who texted you?"

"A friend." Oh, my God. Why was I failing today? "Just a friend" was code for more than that in Snow's book.

"Eight! You have a…boy-girl-they friend?"

I had to laugh because with me, you never knew who I'd gravitate toward.

"A guy, but I don't think we're boyfriends."

"Christopher, Simon has a boyfriend," I heard him shout, and I would put money on the fact that everyone in a ten-mile radius now thought I had a boyfriend.

"Who?" Pops's voice was menacing, but he sort of always sounded that way. "What's his full name? We can do a background check on him."

"Okay, I'm ending the call."

"Wait," Snow said.

"Love you guys."

"Simon, don't you dare—"

And I ended the call.

I immediately read the text from Rush, not giving Snow or Pops a second thought.

Hey. You have time today? I wanted to talk to you about something, after four thirty would be great.

Worry and curiosity battled for dominance. What could he want to talk to me about?

I have one more class at three then I'm done, so after four thirty works.

Perfect. I'll let you know where.

I slid the phone into my pocket, grabbed my bag, and left my dorm for my last class.

———

We ended up not meeting until seven. He'd asked me to join him at the Art Center. It was truly a remarkable building; the walls were all murals painted by graduates of the university. My favorite was one of a man standing on a rock, looking out toward the ocean as a mermaid burst through the water. It was so realistic, and the expression on the man's face showed he was in love. He was there for her and she for him.

I wasn't sure exactly where Rush wanted to meet me here, but I didn't mind searching for him. As I walked the halls, that same feeling that I was being watched came over me. I stopped and turned abruptly. No one was there, but I could not ignore the feeling. It sort of echoed what Snow had said earlier about how I needed to watch my professors for tells, to get to know who they were. I needed to follow this feeling.

Retracing my steps from where I came, making sure to be extra quiet, I walked all the way to the mermaid mural and never bumped into anyone. But the feeling was still there.

Maybe I was crazy? I took out my phone and texted Rush.

I'm here, where are you?

At this point I had wasted so much time chasing ghosts, I didn't want him to think I'd bailed on him.

Room 34.

I had been so close to where he was before I decided to track some phantom stalker.

Be there in a few.

I booked it to where he was, the hair on the back of my neck standing on end.

I heard the tinkling of piano keys as I got closer to where Rush had told me he was. The door was open and when I entered, he was positioned facing away from me. He was really into the music. I leaned against the doorjamb and listened. I knew the tune as a famous song, and damn, he was outstanding. I'd seen him performing at The Falsetto Café the other night, but this was different, more relaxed. It was as if I were witnessing a private piece of him.

I suddenly wished I could introduce Rush to Adelaide, the daughter of Snow's friend Poe, so they could play together. She's phenomenal with the piano. I had never wanted anyone to meet my family. What was it about this man that did that to me?

Slowly, I moved closer until I was behind him—not so close

that he'd get distracted, but I wanted to see his fingers. They flew over the keys, damn near danced as if they'd imprinted on the piano.

When he finished I heard him take a deep breath, as if playing that song gave him life. He had so much passion for music and entertaining; I could not understand how he could push it aside for something his father wanted.

"Hey." I knew there was no way he wasn't going to jump, so I made sure to speak softly.

"Hi, how long have you been here?"

I sat beside him on the bench and placed my hand over one of his that were splayed on the keys. "Long enough to know that music is your life, and this is where you should be."

He gave me a small smile. "We talked about this. I can't expect you to understand the sacrifices I have to make for my family."

I'd never wanted so strongly to tell someone about who I was. I thought for a moment that maybe I could. Pops would agree—I was sure...right? I opened my mouth to say something but was interrupted when someone walked into the room. I assumed they were lost, but they stormed right over to Rush. Instinctively I stood, went around the bench, and blocked the guy.

"Who the hell are you?" I pressed my hand against his chest.

"You'd be wise to remove your hand." The man narrowed his eyes.

"And you'd be wise not to come in here looking like you're about to start shit."

"Simon." I heard Rush stand and move next to me. "It's okay."

"Simon?" The man glared at Rush. "Is he a student here?"

"He is, Father."

Father? *Oh, fuck. Fuck, fuck, fuck.*

"Simon, what?" he asked, and I removed my hand.

"Mancia," I answered. "I'm sorry I came at you, but you looked sort of murderous and were coming at Rush like you were gonna hit him, and I just reacted."

"Reacted? You oftentimes find yourself standing between people and perceived danger?"

He had no idea. "Occasionally. So, sorry."

"Hmm." I knew that expression well; that was disgust. I guessed any chance of impressing Rush's family was gone.

"Why are you here?" Rush maneuvered himself between me and his father.

"I heard you made a spectacle in the cafeteria today. My phone wouldn't stop ringing, and students were informing me—"

"You mean student, one in particular. The one I warned to leave me alone or I'd report him. Yeah, I told him loudly, and I did that so people would witness it."

"Someone's harassing you?" Tendrils of anger climbed up my spine.

"This does not concern you; it's a family matter." Rush's father waved me away as if I were some annoying gnat.

Normally I'd react, but I didn't want to make things harder for Rush, so I stepped back and let them talk.

"Regardless if it was one student or ten, it's unacceptable. Especially from an Abernathy."

"I'm not letting someone bother me and doing nothing about it at the risk of a name, Father. I tasked you to talk to your guard dog about coming near me."

"I did speak with him and will again but nevertheless, you have a duty to me, this school, and our name to uphold, honor, and respect. This matter is closed for now."

"Because you say so?"

Rush's father quirked a brow, a grim expression adorning his face. "Precisely."

He shot me one more withering look and left the room.

After a beat, Rush seemed awkward and embarrassed. "So, that's my dad."

I wasn't sure what to say to that, so I simply said, "Charming."

CHAPTER EIGHT

Rush

I did not want to discuss what had just happened with my father, but Simon wasn't letting it go so easily.

"Is someone harassing you?"

"It's not harassing me in the sense that he'll hurt me—he's annoying is all."

"How so?"

I sat back on the piano bench and Simon joined me. It was snug, but I liked having him close.

"As you can imagine, my father has some serious clout here at the university, and getting on his good side could only be good for you, understand?"

"I understand that being in the good graces of someone with power is beneficial, yeah."

"This guy is so desperate for my father's approval, he thinks by ratting on me it will show my father what a huge asset he is or something. He's so far up his ass, I don't know how my father even sits down."

"And what happened in the cafeteria?"

"Personally, I think he was upset because my father got angry with him. It's like he can't function if he's hated by him." I shrugged. Trying to figure out the inner workings of Fred's mind was scary.

"You should point him out to me."

I smiled, warmed by his concern. "So you can get all tough with him like you did my father?"

Simon appeared ashamed. "I'm sorry about that. I didn't know. He walked in here all explosive, making a beeline for you, and I reacted."

"It's okay, even sweet."

"I'll be sure to apologize again to him."

"No need, but how about I tell you why I wanted to talk to you?"

"Okay, shoot."

As I sat there telling Simon all about the talent show thing Em had asked me to be part of, he smiled and nodded excitedly, taking in my words. I told him all about Trans Lifeline and the auction, and he truly seemed excited about it…for me.

"That's so great, Rush. And I'll absolutely be there cheering you on."

I kissed him quickly, knowing I could not be making out with him at the Art Center; my father would have my hide.

"I don't know what to auction. Em suggested a night at The Falsetto Café, lessons, what do you think?"

"Me?"

"Yeah, what would you do?"

Simon appeared to be deep in thought, and a small smile played on his lips. I wanted to know what he was thinking at that exact moment.

"My dad, he loves to perform. It's nothing like on Broadway or anything, but one time he and I did this Lady Gaga routine at my school. He dressed up exactly like her, and I have to admit the similarities were shocking. Anyway, I found I liked getting on stage with him and performing. Now, I don't do that much anymore; it's not my passion."

"That's an adorable story, but I'm not sure I understand what you're suggesting."

"What about auctioning off a chance to do a show with you at the café? There are a lot of art majors here and others who would love to just entertain with you."

I furrowed my brow. "You think people would pay to do that?"

"I honest-to-God do."

I rattled that idea around in my head. I would have to talk to Luis to see if he would be all right with me offering something like that. I knew people loved watching me perform, but I'd never really thought they would want to do it with me.

"So you think I should do it?"

"You fucking better," Simon joked.

It had been such a long time since I'd shared my passion with someone who appreciated and encouraged it. This time when I kissed Simon, it was not quick.

———

The following day I felt lighter than I had in a while, and I could not stop smiling. I'd called Luis last night after I got back to my dorm, too excited to sleep. He was thrilled to hear I was doing something with "my talent."

I contacted Em, who was also thrilled, and whenever I wasn't in classes, I found myself thinking about what I'd do for the show and what performances I'd do with whoever won the auction.

It was close to dinnertime when I got a phone call from my father telling me he wanted to have breakfast with me in the morning at the Golden Tulip. It was the most pretentious restaurant in town, so naturally that was where he'd demanded we meet.

It was pointless to reject him, and he'd obviously seen my schedule and knew I didn't have a class before the afternoon. I hadn't heard from Simon all day, but I suspected he had a full class load and when we'd parted ways last night, he'd said he was planning something for our date this weekend. I'd simply have to wait until then.

As I entered the cafeteria, Fred was leaving and fortunately didn't notice me. I heard him say to whomever he was talking to on the phone that he would be right there and could not wait. I knew very little about Fred, but I had never seen him with anyone on campus in the three years we had both been here. Either way, I knew I would be able to eat in peace without him bothering me.

I scanned the cafeteria for Simon. A few people noticed me and waved, and one asked how my classes were.

"Great, yours?" As he spoke, I continued searching for Simon.

The guy—I couldn't remember his name—walked away, and I was alone...and there was no Simon. Jesus, I needed to chill. He had a life, and I couldn't expect him to always be wherever I was.

"Hey, Rush." I looked over and saw Penelope in line behind me.

"Hi."

"Eating alone, no Simon?" She waggled her eyebrows and we both chuckled.

"Just grabbing a salad and a burger, I'll go eat in my dorm. I'm exhausted and it's been a long day."

She shrugged. "Or you can eat with me."

I didn't want to hurt her feelings, and I knew she was friends with Simon, so I nodded and after getting our food, we sat at a small table by the window.

"How long have you known Simon?" I asked as I poured dressing on my salad.

"I met him last year at orientation, actually. We flirted a bit and then a couple of weeks later, he asked me out. But that only lasted six months. We weren't good together."

"I'm sorry." I didn't want to pry. But I'd be lying if I didn't wonder why they weren't compatible.

"Nah, we're just better as friends. And, between the two of us, I wasn't joking the other night when I said he was really secretive. I've never seen his family, he avoids all questions about home, and whenever it starts to get personal, he dodges and weaves and the next thing you know, you're talking about yourself."

She didn't seem bitter—matter of fact, perhaps.

"Maybe he doesn't talk about it because it's too painful." I wanted to give Simon the benefit of the doubt, and it felt wrong to speak of him when he wasn't here.

"No. What I have gained from Simon is that he loves his family and has had a fairy-tale life."

I thought about what I did know regarding Simon. He didn't give off any vibes that he was struggling, and he had mentioned his dads to me in a positive way. I wondered why he didn't speak in depth about them.

"He's a great guy, Rush, and I think he really likes you. Don't think I'm saying any of this out of jealousy or anything, because I'm not. I have a great boyfriend now. I'm just letting you know that it'll be hard breaking down those walls."

I smiled at her. "Thanks for the heads-up."

CHAPTER NINE

Simon

I spent my morning trying to find some book in the library I had forgotten to buy, and now there were none left at the bookstore. When I went to download it off Amazon, of course it was not the version the professor wanted. Fortunately, someone told me I would find it here. I was approaching the counter with the book to sign it out, when I saw Rush's father outside. He moved with purpose toward the administrative building, which made sense, though I didn't know exactly what Rush's father actually did for the university.

I had a few classes, but afterward I wanted to go to his office and apologize to him. Normally, I wouldn't give a flying fuck since men like him did not deserve respect. But I really liked Rush, and I wanted to make things easier for him.

When my last class was done, I looked at my watch and realized it was close to dinnertime, and I hadn't spoken to Rush all day. I figured I would wait until after my conversation with his father.

I hiked my bag up on my shoulder and made my way over to

the administrative building. The directory read that Rushmore Abernathy the Second was on the third floor. Thankfully, there was an elevator, because my legs were feeling the burn from moving all over throughout the day.

As I got off on the third floor, I was surprised that most of the lights were off in the offices, but they were probably done for the day, or there were not a lot of people on this floor.

When I reached the end of the hallway, I saw an office door with frosted glass. It was illuminated, and the sign on the door simply read his name, no title.

I raised my hand to knock, but the sound of a voice on the other side stopped me.

"I specifically told you not to confront my son."

"I'm sorry, sir, but you were so cross with me, and I panicked. I knew you told me not to go and say any more but...I hate when you're mad at me."

I lowered my hand and listened. I knew Rush's father's voice but didn't recognize who the other guy was, and with the frosted glass I couldn't see. I moved to the side so no one would catch sight of my shadow.

"And how do you think I'm currently feeling when you deliberately disobeyed me after I specifically told you no?"

"Disappointed?" the other voice said.

"Beyond even that, boy."

Boy? What the...?

"You need to be punished." Rush's father's tone deepened, and I could hear the dark promise in it. It felt as if a rock had dropped in the pit of my stomach. No way was this happening.

"How will I be punished?"

"Drop your pants, hands on the table."

I should have left, I really should have, but my feet wouldn't let me. I was glued in place. Not to mention this was Rush's father, and I had a feeling the person in that room was a student here and obviously the asshole who had been harassing Rush.

I looked up and down the hallway, but there was no one here—just me and this awkward situation. As much as I did not want to listen, I needed to see who the person in the room was, and to do that I needed to wait until they left.

I put my phone on silent in case I got a call or text, and I did a quick sweep of my surroundings. The office across from Rush's father's was vacant and dark. The door was open, so I'd be able to run over there in a pinch.

"Spread your cheeks and let me see your tight little hole," Rush's father urged, and I tried not to throw up. "Good." I heard a slap and a gasp. "Let's make this hole nice and red; then I'll fuck you, and you'll carry my come in your ass with a plug all day tomorrow. You'll be sore and uncomfortable. But you'll remember what happens when you upset Daddy."

My stomach churned. Maybe it would've been hot in a porn or whatever, but this was not doing it for me.

"I'm sorry," the guy pleaded.

I heard a series of slaps and gasps. "Keep your hole on display!"

"Sorry, Daddy."

I had heard enough; I couldn't just stand there. I went over to the other office and waited. I could tell they were fucking from the sounds that echoed through the vacant hallway. Every part of me was spinning. Rage rippled over my skin, as waves of nausea crashed through me. Clenching my fists, I breathed in and out slowly to control my temper. I couldn't fly off the handle and storm in there. So, I waited and tried to chill the fuck out.

The fact was, Rush's father was having a sexual relationship with someone who was making his son's life a living hell, and I needed to know who it was. All thoughts of apologizing to Rush's dad went out the window. Now I wanted to see who had the nerve to harass Rush.

My phone lit up a few times, once from Snow, but it went to voice mail; I'd listen later. Once from Rush, saying he was in for the night and wanted to see how my day was. I could not say fine....I mean I could, but that would be a lie. I ignored it because I had to think about what the fuck I was going to do here.

While I sat there, waiting for the horror from across the hall to end, I made sure my flash wasn't on. *On second thought, it might be better to do a video of whoever is in there as they're leaving...*

My phone kept lighting up, two more times from Snow and another from Pops. It was very unlike me to not answer them, so I had zero doubt they thought I was kidnapped and being tortured...Yeah, this was the life I was born into; that thought process wasn't unrealistic.

I shot off a text to Snow that I was in the middle of something and would call in a little while.

Then I heard the door creak open, and I hit record on my phone.

"Now, be a good boy and if you are, tomorrow night I'll remove the plug." The sound of Rush's dad's voice made me jump.

I inched the phone from behind the door so that only the lens was poking out. I could see Rush's father's back.

"Yes, Daddy." The other person didn't seem upset; there was a thrill of excitement in his tone, and finally the mystery man came into view.

I recognized him as the creep who'd been staring at me the other night in the cafeteria, and I was also pretty sure he worked in the bookstore.

"Get out of here." Rush's dad slapped bookstore guy on the ass. What was his name?

I waited until the office door shut again and the man was

headed down the elevator before coming out of my hiding spot. What I held in my hand was ammo to stop the harassment for Rush and even blackmail to make his dad leave him be, too. But it was also devastation for Rush. I was sure if he ever saw this, he'd be heartbroken.

I slid the phone into my pocket and got out of that building in a hurry. I really wished Snow and Pops were here to give me advice, but I knew if I asked for it, it very well might mean someone would come here to help me figure it out, and I wasn't sure that's what was best right now.

Any thoughts of eating dinner were nonexistent. I got to my dorm, shut the door, plopped on my bed, and sadly watched the video to make sure it was all clear. It was, and now I needed to figure out what to do with it.

I could call Snow and ask what he would do in a situation like this, but that would blow up in my face because he'd say, "Is someone blackmailing you?" and my pops would come here and send the Haven Hart Mafia to Abernathy University, and there would be a war. No, I needed to try and figure this out on my own. I did need to return Snow's call, though.

I cleared my throat and called him.

"I want you to know Christopher was strapping guns to his body and on the phone with Bill, Mace, and Frank, telling them to be on standby to take a chopper to your university when you didn't answer us." This was how Snow was choosing to say hello.

"Do you not see how irrational that is?"

"You never ignore our calls. Anyone can get your phone and text for you. When you don't answer and we don't hear your voice, it's terrifying."

He was not wrong. "Okay, but I am a grown-up, and I do have this crazy thing called a life."

"Simon." When Snow used my name, I knew it was serious. "You're not just any adult, you're the heir to the Manos throne, and you know it. You're the weak link in Christopher's armor. If anyone got to you and hurt you...I don't even want to think about it."

"I know, I'm sorry."

"At least tell me you were doing something good?"

I was never so glad that Snow couldn't see my face as I answered. "It was certainly something I'll never forget."

He sighed. "Oh, the college life. I wish I had that experience. But alas, that was not my destiny. I'll live vicariously through you. Tell me all about this thing you'll never forget, because I know a thing or two about never forgetting."

It was true; Snow had a photographic and eidetic memory—he remembered everything.

"I actually have a ton of homework to do, can I take a rain check?" I did have assignments to complete so that wasn't a lie, and I had to figure out what I was going to do with this video and the knowledge of what Rush's father was doing.

"Of course, college man. I'll talk to you later. Love you."

I disconnected the call, smashed my face into the pillow on my bed, and screamed.

CHAPTER TEN

Rush

Entering the Golden Tulip was like walking into an opulent nightmare filled with gold, crystal, and white tulips so pure you knew they had to be made in a lab somewhere.

"Good morning, sir, do you have a reservation?" The hostess smiled, her perfectly white teeth on display and cherry-red lips arched in a fake kind of happiness.

"The table is under Abernathy."

She nodded. "Oh yes, follow me, please."

Of course, my father wanted our table to be in some alcove somewhere away from anyone who'd dare hear either one of us say something that could taint the good Abernathy name.

"Ah, Rushmore, good morning." My father's smile was strained, proving he was faking his happiness for the benefit of the hostess.

"Morning," I grumbled and took my seat.

Once the hostess was gone, the server took our drink and food orders, and unfortunately, we were alone.

Before my father had a chance to control the conversation, I figured I'd step in. "Have you spoken to Fred?"

He appeared taken aback. Had he forgotten why we were meeting today?

"I told you the other day I had."

"No, you told him, and he still came at me. You then said you'd be sure to speak with him again. Or would it just be easier if I filed a complaint?" I raised my brows, feeling brave.

"I spoke with him again last night. I assure you he will stay out of your way, but, Rushmore, these public displays, they must end. And who is this Simon you're hanging out with?"

"Father, you do know I'll be twenty-two in a few months, right? Who I hang out with or date is none of your concern. And as for the outbursts when it comes to Fred, that was on him."

He rolled his eyes. "Yes, well, I was referring to the angry outbursts but also the singing. I understand—"

"We spoke about this already too. Why am I here? I feel like you're beating a dead horse with these conversations."

My father sighed. "Rushmore, you're becoming unruly. When you started college we spoke about your future, and you said you understood your responsibility as an Abernathy. I feel you're going astray."

"See, this is where we see a single event differently." I shook my head at him.

"How?"

"You told me what I'd major in if I wanted a college education. You ordered me to live up to the name; there was no discussion. If I had it my way, I'd be an arts major, not English. But, no, art was...what did you say? 'Too queer an image.' Well, news flash, I'm gay! Kinda all the queer, right over here." I pointed at myself.

You'd have thought I'd incited a riot, the way my father's eyes scanned the room, ready to explain my outburst.

"Rushmore, this is what I'm talking about. Perhaps it's not I who misunderstood our conversation three years ago, but you."

I was about to stand up and leave when the server came by with our food.

"Okay, gentlemen, here's your breakfasts." My father and I were shooting daggers at each other, unbeknownst to the server. "If there's anything else, please don't hesitate to let me know." With a quick smile, he was gone.

"Perhaps the company you're keeping isn't so wise." He narrowed his eyes.

I reached into my pocket to pull out my wallet. "You're the one that has a harassing nutjob stalking me, and you're going to criticize who I hang out with?" I huffed and tossed three twenties on the table. "I'm done with this father-son bonding shit for a while." Without waiting for a response, I got up and stormed out.

Even though I had not heard from Simon and I had no idea what classes he had today, the urge to see and talk to him was overwhelming. So, I let my legs do the decision-making. I asked someone as I entered the building if they knew what room Simon was in, and I was glad when one of the resident advisors did. When I was in front of his dorm room, I knocked.

I heard some shuffling followed by the door opening. A sleep-rumpled Simon stood before me. He only had on boxers and a small smile. But when his eyes widened in surprise, I realized perhaps he was hoping it was someone else.

"I'm sorry for just dropping by."

"What? No, it's fine, come in." He pushed the door wider, and I stepped in. As soon as I heard the click indicating it was just us, I took a deep breath.

"Are you okay?" He stood in front of me, bare chested, and I hadn't realized how cut he was until now. Clearly he worked out. "Rush?"

"Huh? Sorry." I pinched the bridge of my nose to relieve some pressure. "I had an almost breakfast with my father. He's such an asshole, and I'm not sure sometimes if I'm going crazy or he is."

"Um…what's an almost breakfast?"

I looked up at him and chuckled. "I never even got to eat the food before walking out."

"I see." He stepped away and was moving toward his dresser. "Are you here to see if I want to go eat with you?"

"What? No, but, I mean okay, sure."

He slipped on a red shirt and turned to me. "I'm sorry your father is so awful, I am. But I think the more you stand up to him and assert who you are, he'll listen."

Something was off about Simon, I couldn't put my finger on it, but he was almost too formal. "What's wrong with you?"

He pulled out a pair of jeans and started putting them on. "Nothing, tired. I have class in like two hours."

"How was class yesterday?" I did not want to sound clingy by asking why we hadn't talked the other day, so this seemed benign.

"Long."

One-word answer, hmm. "Did you crash early?"

He grabbed a tube of toothpaste and a toothbrush. "I did, be right back. I have to go brush my teeth."

He left the room, and I hated the nagging feeling that he was hiding something. I mean, I knew so little about Simon, that was likely it. I walked around his room, realizing quickly that there was not one photo of his family. Even I had a picture of me, my dad, and my mother. He had a few posters and a large calendar but nothing indicating where he lived. No trophies, old-school sweatshirt, nothing.

"Okay, sorry about that." His smile fell when he looked at me. "What is it?"

"There's not one personal thing in your room. Not a photo or anything. I mean, I don't get along with my dad, but I have a picture of me, him, and my mom in there."

"You have a mom?" He sounded genuinely shocked.

"Yes, what did you think, I was hatched?"

He closed his eyes and took a breath. "Sorry, that was a dumb question. You never talk about her."

I shrugged away the pain. "She died four years ago. Not much to tell, really. She was depressed so much, and I guess…well, the darkness won. My dad found her in their bedroom; she shot herself."

"Shit, Rush." He came over to me and engulfed me in probably the best hug I'd ever had. "I'm so sorry."

"It's okay, but I'm liking the hug."

He gave me one last squeeze before letting go. "You can have a hug anytime, just ask, or hell, grab me and we will do it right there…maybe in front of your dad, *dun dun dunnnn*."

I laughed and playfully slapped his chest. "Dork."

"Yeah, okay, seriously, I'm starving, and I have class in an hour and a half now. Let's go to the cafeteria."

I nodded and followed him out. It wasn't until we were halfway through breakfast, having talked about the latest twist on a show we both loved, that I realized he'd evaded the entire subject of him having no photos or nothing personal in his room. How did he do that, and who was Simon Mancia?

With everything going on between my father and me and wondering if becoming an art major was even a possibility now, even if it enraged dear old Dad, I was massively intrigued by Simon and his many secrets.

CHAPTER ELEVEN

Simon

Evading questions about myself was getting harder and harder to do with Rush. The whole purpose of me not telling anyone I was actually a Manos was for their, and my, safety. But that was because I thought if anyone got hold of that information, they would never be able to keep it to themselves. I'd only known Rush for a short time, and I was sure my pops would think I was insane for trusting him, but Rush felt different.

The only thing I worried about was him informing his father, not maliciously, but regardless of anything or how he felt about the man, he was still his dad. And after hearing what had happened to Rush's mother, I couldn't help wondering if his dad was having some midlife crisis and that was why he was having sex with a student.

I was so messed up in my head over what to do. Should I tell Rush what I saw? If I didn't and he found out on his own and told me, I couldn't deny it. And then I would have to deal with him feeling deceived by me.

"Where are you?" Rush gently nudged my shoulder as we walked toward our classes.

"Sorry, just thinking about a project I have to do, and my mind is all over the place."

"Understandable, I get that way too."

"I have a question for you, something you might know with your extensive knowledge of this university."

He smiled. "Oh, Lord. Okay, hit me."

"Does this school have a policy on staff or teachers dating students?"

Rush stopped walking and stared at me with utter puzzlement. "Are you asking for yourself?"

I burst out laughing. "God, no. Let's just say I sort of know someone that's having a sexual relationship with a staff member here. It got me thinking."

He nodded and continued walking. "Well, the policy here at Abernathy states that a professor can't have any relationship with a student if they are teaching them or if that student has to answer to them for anything. The dean is prohibited from any relationship with any student per Abernathy's policies, I believe. Make sense?"

"It does, unless the dean's wife or whatever took a course here, what then?"

"Huh, I don't know. Interesting. So, this friend of yours, are they having a relationship with a professor?"

I shook my head. "They're administration, I think. I mean they work here, but I don't know their title."

"And you can't tell me who because it'll break the confidence you have with your friend."

I was glad he understood…even if that was not why I didn't want him to know.

"Honestly, I don't even know what half these administrators

and staff do." I chuckled, trying to work my way into asking what his father did.

"We have heads of departments like Art, English, History, things like that. Most of them are also professors as well. We have IT, the CIO, CFO, Vice President of Finance. I mean the list goes on. There's a directory right online you can look up."

I had searched the directory but never saw his father mentioned. I didn't want to pry further and risk him figuring out I knew something about his dad.

"You should maybe talk to your friend, though. Even if it's allowed by policy, it's awfully frowned upon and whoever that administrator or whoever it is, they'll be ostracized horribly. My father would see to that. He'd sell his soul if it meant Abernathy University was always held to a stellar standard."

I could not believe the irony of this situation. Rush and I split on the pathway for him to head to his class and me to mine. I wished everything he said to me had helped to clear up my fuzzy head, but it didn't. I was as confused as ever.

By the end of my classes, I had a colossal headache, and I wasn't sure if it was all the knowledge I'd retained or the dilemma with Rush's father. I had no one here to talk to about it.

The clock read eleven at night. I knew there was always a possibility Snow was asleep, but it wouldn't matter; he would see it was me and be up like a shot. I hated to do it, but I needed advice.

I plumped my pillows up, sat back, and called.

"Hello, Eight?" Snow sounded on guard, probably because I never called at this hour.

"Hey, Snow."

There was a beat of silence before he spoke. "What's wrong?"

"Is that Simon? Something happen?" I heard Pops; his voice was heavy with sleep, so I knew I had woken them both up.

"Yes, it's Simon, but I think he's fine…You're fine, right?"

"Sort of, I have a dilemma and sort of need advice."

"It's okay, Chris, it's not life threatening…Put your fucking phone down. I swear, if you call Bill and all of them every time Simon calls, they won't come when you actually need them!"

I chuckled because I could totally see this playing out. My pops sometimes worried more than Snow did.

"Okay, Eight, I'm all ears, let it out."

I took a deep breath and spilled everything to Snow. All about Rush, how we met, the harassment he'd been getting, Rush's mother, and the sex I'd witnessed. I left nothing out since if I was going to get advice, he needed to know everything.

When I finished, uninterrupted, I waited. Hell, I hoped Snow had all the answers for me.

"Oh, sweet boy, that's a lot to unpack."

It really was. "I just don't know what to do, and it's not like there's anyone here I can talk to, especially Rush."

As I sat in bed I turned my hand over and traced along my tattoo of the infinity symbol…At least that was what anyone who looked at it would think—in reality it was the number eight and my forever reminder of home.

"You're calling for advice, and I will give it to you but, Eight, this advice is not based on a regular person's life. You need to know, you're not an average person holding on to this information."

I did know that. Everything I did reflected on the Manos name, and everyone here knew me as Simon Mancia.

"I know."

"Okay, in order to know what exactly the safe thing to do is, Simon…" He sighed. "We need to know who these people are."

"You want to do background checks." It was not a question, and I'd known it was coming.

"It's how we live; it's how we survive." I knew Snow was right, and I hated it.

"Thing is, I don't know who the guy with Rush's father is. I mean he works at the bookstore, so I might be able to find out."

"Fair enough. Until then, Eight, do nothing. We can run some background on the Abernathys. I know this is hard for you and you wanted the best advice, so I won't leave you without something, so here it goes. Be there for Rush right now, encourage his passions and care about him how you do. I understand a huge part of you wants to tell him what you saw, and it will come to that, I believe so, but until we know what kind of beast lives in that cave, you can only wait and be the Eight I know you to be."

"Thanks, Snow. I will, and I'll see if I can get that bookstore guy's name."

"I love you, Eight…so, so much."

I went to sleep that night not feeling any better. I was still going to have to lie to Rush, and I hated it. As I lay in bed, staring at the ceiling, I wondered…if the man Rush's father was fucking hadn't been the same person harassing him, would I even care? I mean they were both adults, right?

"Fuck!" I shouted into the empty room.

Rush and I had our date coming up, and I had to get my shit together. Too many times I'd watched my pops put on an expressionless face, even though I knew he was terrified inside. I could be that person.

I would be that person.

CHAPTER TWELVE

Rush

I hadn't seen much of Simon since the other day at breakfast, and tonight was our date. He'd texted me this morning telling me he would pick me up around seven and to get ready for an amazing night.

Simon was acting strange, and I swore he was avoiding me, but the start of every school year was hectic, and I decided to cut him some slack.

I spent the rest of the week circumventing my father, fortunately not seeing Fred anywhere. Was it wishful thinking that my father had actually come through and forced Fred to stop?

An hour before Simon was to pick me up, I sat in my dorm, getting ready, when the phone rang. The phone my father forced me to have.

"Hello, Father," I answered listlessly.

"I'm sorry to say this is not your father; is this Rushmore Abernathy the Third?"

No one called this number except my father. I didn't think anyone else even knew it.

"Who is this?"

"You can call me Bic."

"Bic? Like the pen company? What the hell is this? What's going on?"

The person, Bic, I guess his name was, became agitated. "I'm just calling to tell you to end your snoopin'; it won't go the way you're thinkin' if you don't."

"Snooping? What are you talking about? Who are you?" I would swear he had the wrong number had he not said my name at the beginning of the call.

Bic laughed darkly on the other end. "I've seen your GPA, don't play stupid. End it, or I end you." And then he hung up.

Without hesitation, the second the creepy guy hung up, I called my father. He answered on the third ring.

"Rushmore?" I was sure he was shocked to hear from me since I never called him.

"Yeah, look, I just got a strange call on the phone you gave me for my dorm...You know, the one only you call me on?"

"Okay, was it a wrong number?"

"No, the guy, he said his name was Bic, told me to stop snooping, and he knew who I was. I don't know what he's talking about, snooping? Did you give that number to anyone, do you even know what's going on?"

There was a beat of silence before he spoke. "Bic? Like the pen company?"

"That's all you have to say? But, yeah, like the pen company."

"I'm sorry, Rushmore. I have no idea what that's about. I can see what I can dig up on campus. But I think it prudent we change that number."

He knew nothing. "Whatever, I have to go. I have a date, but if you can figure out what the guy was talking about, that would be great. He spoke in finalities, Father. Like the *stop or you die* kind of finalities."

I could practically hear his eyes widening, if that were possible. "Perhaps we should call the authorities."

"And tell them what, a giant pen man pranked me?"

"Filing a report is wise; it begins a paper trail and if someone is threatening you and God forbid you're harmed, this report could get them locked up."

I could admit to myself only that he had a good point. "Fine, I'll do it in the morning."

"Because you have a date?"

"Yes, a date."

"Hmm. Is it with that Simon fella?" There was no hiding the disdain in his tone.

"Yes."

"And you think shenanigans with Simon is smarter than reporting this to the police?"

"Look, I didn't call for a lecture. I called to see if you knew anything and you clearly don't, so I'm going now. Have a good night."

"Rushmo—"

I hung up before I could hear what he had to say. It wouldn't matter; it was surely something awful about Simon.

I finished getting ready for my date, but my mind was preoccupied the whole time. I found myself thinking about every activity I'd been doing and if something I'd done had been misconstrued as snooping. I was halfway to paranoid by the time Simon knocked on my door.

I took a deep breath, painted a smile on my face, and opened the door. I was not going to have anything ruin a night I had been looking forward to.

He smiled at me and damn, it was his best accessory for sure. The outfit hugged his body in all the right places, though, and I would be lying if I didn't say there wasn't a sort of power around him. I'd never noticed it before, and it might not even be intentional, but he commanded a room.

"You look amazing," I said.

"Shit, you took my line. Hang on…" He tapped his chin and I laughed. "You look outstanding."

"Mmhmm, gonna one-up me, are you?" I grabbed my wallet and stepped out of my room.

"Every chance I get."

We talked about our day—our week, actually—as I followed him out. I knew he was driving since he'd organized the date, and I wasn't paying much attention until we got to the car.

"This is your car?" My eyes widened. I didn't know a lot about cars, but this was the newest Mercedes Benz out there.

"It is…What's wrong?" He seemed confused. My father made a lot of money, and we lived a good life, but even he had never owned a Mercedes AMG GT Black Series…and Simon was a college student.

"It's just…wow! This car is…" I released a breath, unsure of what to say.

"Oh, is it a bit much? It was a gift, no way I could afford this on my own, okay, yeah, so let's get going." He held the door open for me, which I thought was sweet, and he was avoiding talking about his life…again.

Simon drove for about forty minutes and the whole time, I was trying to figure out where he was taking us. Every time I released a frustrated growl he laughed.

Finally, he turned, and I saw this huge lit-up piano on the top of a building. The sign below it read The Key Tone Brothers.

"What is this place? I've never seen it."

He chuckled and drove along a circle where a valet came to his side of the car.

"Two brothers own this place, and they are pianists who compete against each other. And you can eat dinner while they perform. I figured it would be a fun date." He got out and I followed.

I watched as he gave the valet his keys and took a yellow ticket in exchange. When he came over to me, I smiled. "This is already the coolest date I've ever been on."

"Let's go see if these guys are better than you are." He took my hand in his, and we stepped inside the building.

My senses were immediately caressed by the sounds of music, the smells of delicious food, and the lights and all-around dazzling atmosphere.

Chandeliers dripped glittering crystals, and the lobby was filled with music-inspired art. Simon walked us over to the hostess station, which was actually a music stand, and I was excited to find all the hidden gems of this place.

"Good evening." The host grinned. "Do you have a reservation?"

"Yes, it's under Simon Mancia."

The host grabbed two menus. "Right this way."

The dining room was humongous; there was no other word to describe it. All the tables were set around a large circular stage where two grand pianos sat—one black, another white. It was marvelous.

"Enjoy your meal and the show." He placed the menus on the table as Simon and I took our seats.

"I can't believe I never knew about this place." I could hear the awe in my voice.

"I went down to the music department and spoke to the head over there. I told them I wanted to take someone out who loved music, but I also wanted to feed them." He laughed and my smile made my face ache. "So, he recommended this place and when I looked it up, I was sold."

"You went to all that work?"

He shrugged as if to play off that it was no big deal, but after the day I'd had, it felt like so much.

"Thanks, Simon."

He didn't get to respond. The server came over to take our orders, and then the show began. The food was mouthwatering, and the performance was breathtaking. It was one hundred percent true that this was the best date I had ever been on, and I intended to show Simon just how much I loved it when he brought me home.

CHAPTER THIRTEEN

Simon

I learned that the guy who worked at the bookstore—the one harassing Rush—was named Fred Brennan. I sent the message over to Snow as soon as I found out and was told to hang tight.

Of course it made the week drag, and by the time my date with Rush came, I was stressed. But all it took was seeing how much he loved The Key Tone Brothers and that smile on his face to wipe away all my worries at least for the night.

Afterward, while Rush and I were waiting outside for the valet to bring my car, Rush went on and on about all the things he'd loved about the performance and the food. I grinned, and just as I saw my car coming up the drive, someone called my name.

"Simon?"

I turned and came face to face with someone from home, and if that wasn't the worst thing to happen to me right now, nothing was.

"Danny?" I had known Danny for a long time. He was a really

troubled kid but with the help of Snow, Pops, and myself he'd gotten straightened out, and last I'd heard he was performing with a band. To see him standing in front of me almost took my breath away.

"Hell, yeah! Damn, look at you!" He laughed, and I could admit he looked great. Happy and healthy. "I can't believe I'm seeing you here."

I needed to get away from this situation. "Um, Danny, this is Rush."

Danny flicked his eyes Rush's way, and a momentary frown appeared on Danny's face before he covered it up. "Nice to meet you."

"Same." Rush shook his hand, and I knew he was curious.

"What brings you here?" I asked Danny, pushing the conversation toward him.

"I'm playing down the block and Fizz, my bandmate, loves this place so we came. And I'm so fucking glad I did." He wrapped his arms around me and the hug he gave me was bone-crushing. Danny and I'd had a brief relationship, but it wasn't healthy, and we'd parted ways.

"So, you know Simon from home?" I knew Rush was being polite, but I was freaking out.

"Car's here!" I went to the valet and handed him a nice tip and took my keys. "Ready to go, Rush?"

He turned his head and cocked it. "Wait a sec, this is a friend obviously excited to see you." He returned his attention to Danny. "How long has it been since you've seen Simon?"

Danny blew out a breath. "Shit, gotta be a couple of years, right, Simon? I think it was at Chris—"

"Yep, long time ago," I cut him off.

"You okay?" Danny's face showed confusion. "You're actin' all squirrelly."

"What? No, I'm good, just on a date is all." I gestured to Rush.

Danny nodded slowly. "Ah, I see. Okay, but take my number, we need to hang out. I'm down this way every few months. We should catch up." I handed him my phone and ignored how Rush was glaring at me. I was being rude beyond words.

"Thanks, Danny, let me text you so you have my number." That seemed to make my being unpleasant better, because Danny smiled, and Rush appeared less peeved.

"Got it." He looked at his phone.

"We'll talk soon, Danny."

"You bet. Have a good night." He waved and I watched as he went back over to his friends.

I had been driving for a few minutes when Rush spoke. "Simon."

"Uh-huh?"

"Can I ask you a question that I'm sure you'll hate?"

I scoffed. "Well, you make it sound so appealing."

"Sorry, it's just...you cover your identity, and it's becoming incredibly obvious. What are you hiding and why?"

I looked in the rearview mirror and no one was there so at the red light, I gave Rush my full attention.

"Knowing my story isn't...how do I say this? Okay, I'm not hiding *who* I am. What you see is what you get as far as personality and shit. But there are things about my life that I don't talk about because they don't just affect me. My secrets keep people safe."

He bit his lip, and I could see he was trying to piece things together. "You're not in witness protection?"

"Not in the sense of the authorities, no, but I am in a sort of protection."

I checked the mirrors, still glad that no one was there.

"And you not talking about it isn't because you don't trust me?"

"Not at all. If anything, I trust you more than anyone here. But I need you to trust me when I tell you that I will let you in when it's safe to do so."

He nodded and rewarded me with a small smile. "Okay, now one more thing." Rush's grin turned lascivious.

"What is it?"

"I want you to take me to my room, and I want to show you just how much I loved this date."

I laughed, relieved the night was saved, then drove back to the university a hell of a lot faster than the limits allowed.

Rush and I had made out a few times, and I was always left wanting more, and judging by his blown pupils I knew he was too. So when Rush closed the door to his room and pressed up against me in the most perfect attack, I folded right into it.

I felt his hardness alongside my cock, and it sent sparks of pleasure through my whole body.

"We are way overdressed." I grinned at Rush, who was clearly in agreement since he began stripping himself of his clothes. I chuckled and began divesting myself of my own.

We were already breathless by the time we were naked. Rush stood a foot away from me, his chest rising and falling as if he'd run a marathon, and I knew mine was doing the same. It was not out of exertion but rather the need to fuck.

"Holy shit, you're gorgeous." Rush's voice was soft with an underlying growl.

"Get the fuck over here."

He crashed into me, his leg hitched up, and instinctively I

grabbed his thigh to hold him in place. Lips, tongues, and teeth, we were like animals and I loved every second of it.

"Bed." We said it at the same time, tumbling onto Rush's mattress, laughing through kisses.

Rush pinned my arms down and grinned at me. "Let me have my way with you, please."

"How polite. How could I say no?"

When he leaned close, I thought he was going for my mouth, but he pressed his lips against my neck, licked across my Adam's apple, and followed a path he created, stopping when he had my nipple between his teeth, eliciting a hiss from me.

He squeezed my hands before letting go in a way that ordered me to keep them there. Curiosity was what made me obey; I was desperate to see what it felt like to let Rush have his way with me.

He traced lightly over my flesh with his tongue, lower and lower, dipping into my belly button, making me chuckle. But soon enough, I wasn't laughing anymore as he licked along my shaft and gently sucked the head of my cock in his mouth.

"Oh, Rush."

With his gaze locked to mine, he took all of me down his throat. The intensity of him watching me, pulling me into this moment more fiercely than I ever had been, made me almost come right there.

"I want you to fuck me." I could hear the hunger and need in my voice and realized how much I wanted this. He halted his ministrations, eyes on me in silent question. "Really."

He released my cock, and his lips shone with spit. "I'm good if you want to fuck me."

"How do you want it?"

He smiled. "I like…no, I love it either way."

"Next time I'll fuck you, until then…" I spread my legs, loving how Rush's eyes widened. "I want you to fuck me into tomorrow."

In a flash, he was resting between my legs, kissing me breathless. I wrapped my arms around him, pulling him infinitely closer as we grinded our cocks together.

"Shit, Rush, I'm gonna come all over your dick, and I want you inside me, right fucking now."

Before he lifted up he bit my lip. "You taste so good."

"Well, you can suck down my come after you fuck me."

"You have a filthy mouth, Simon...I like it."

He reached over into his nightstand and pulled out lube and a condom.

"I'm on PrEP." He placed the condom on my stomach and sat up, lazily stroking his cock.

"Mmm, I am too, but—"

"No, you're right. I have to admit it's been too long since I was tested. Better to be safe."

I handed him the lube that he'd placed next to me, and with a salacious grin he squeezed some onto his fingers. I watched as he brought them to my hole, and I shivered at the slightest touch. As he worked me open, he devoured my mouth in a scorching kiss. His tongue pumped into me in sync with his fingers, and I could quickly feel myself coming undone.

"Rush," I whispered against his mouth.

"I know." He removed his fingers, and I heard the tearing of the wrapper. It felt like I was floating and vibrating at the same time.

When he slid inside me, slowly, nothing had ever felt more right. I gripped my cock, not jacking it; I didn't want to come. The friction, the burn, the feeling as he pushed inside me and grazed over my prostate...all of it had me arching up.

"Easy, Simon, I got you."

How was he so calm? I wanted him to pound into me and he was so...I opened my eyes, and he was not calm. He was two seconds away from crazy.

"Fuck me, Rush."

I didn't have to ask twice. He put his arms on either side of my body, I wrapped my legs around him, and fuck me he did. Every thrust and slam hit me just right, and there was no way I would be able to hold my orgasm back.

One last slam, and we came. I didn't know if it was Rush who shouted or me, because I fell into oblivion after that.

CHAPTER FOURTEEN

Rush

Waking up wrapped around Simon was the best way to greet the day. I smiled thinking about last night and how I had never connected with someone physically like I did with Simon. This was by far my favorite morning to date.

"What time is it?" Simon's voice was thick with sleep and sexy as all hell.

"Don't know, don't care. It's the weekend."

He chuckled, turning to untangle us, which I wasn't a fan of. "Don't you work?"

"Not this week, but next weekend is the charity open mic night at the café...Think you may want to sing a little?"

He scoffed and playfully slapped my chest. "No, my singing days are over."

That had me sitting up faster than my head liked. "Over? You sang?"

"Chill out, Madonna. I used to do fun acts with one of my dads, remember? Nothing like what you do."

"I need these details, Simon. Don't leave a guy hanging."

He laughed and pushed the covers off his body. "I have to get back to my dorm, actually, because I have a huge exam to study for...Yes, I know it's the beginning of the year, but this professor seems to favor torture so..." He shrugged and got up.

Resting on my pillows, I ogled his every bend and move. "I hate that you're leaving but watching you move, that's entertainment. Bet we could get a lot of charity money if you stood on stage, naked, picking things up."

He pulled his briefs up. "Ha and no."

"What are you doing tonight? We can get dinner or something." I hoped I wasn't sounding needy. But it had been a long time since I'd genuinely enjoyed someone's company.

"Yeah, that's perfect. I can get a lot done in a few hours. I'll text when I'm done." He pulled his shirt on, bent, and gave me a kiss that washed away my fretting that I was clinging. "If you want, stay naked in bed, and I'll join you later."

"Don't tempt me."

With one last kiss, he slipped on his shoes and left my room. I pressed my face into the pillow he'd slept on and fell asleep.

At around noon, I decided I was in need of a grocery store run. I usually ate in the cafeteria or, if I was working, Luis would cook me up something. I liked having some convenient items—such as water, milk, and essentials—so if I didn't want to go anywhere, I didn't have to. I only had a few things and with nothing to do, I put my shoes on and went to stock up.

The store closest to the university was not huge, but it had everything a college student needed to survive. Soda, ramen noodles, mac 'n' cheese...the staples.

I grabbed a small cart and started filling it with what I needed.

I found myself thinking about things maybe Simon would like

when he came over…if he came over. We could watch a movie and—

From the left someone crashed into my cart, and I whipped my head around. "Hey!"

I saw a huge—and I mean *huge*—man. He was well over six foot five, broad, and very out of place in this store.

"Maybe watch where you're going."

His voice…I had heard it before. "You came whipping out of the aisle."

"Did I?" He narrowed his eyes. "I guess I should be careful, so I don't get hurt…or hurt anyone, being so careless and all."

And like cold water to overheated skin, the realization of who this was hit me. "Are you Bic?" *Why did I ask that out loud?*

He shrugged and walked away. What the fuck was going on? I wanted to chase after the guy, but I had to be realistic; he was almost double my size and could flick me into next week.

As quickly as I could, I grabbed what was most important and hightailed it out of there. The second I got in my car I locked it, and it took me a good five minutes to calm myself. I didn't know what this person wanted with me and what he thought I was snooping into. The only thing I could think of was, this had to do with my father, and this Bic dude was confusing us.

As soon as I returned to my room, I called my father but it went to voice mail, so I left a message.

"I think something is going on. That guy who called me yesterday threatening me found me in the supermarket today and crashed into my cart. You said you'd see if you could find out anything with the university, so any information you have would be a great thing. Call me back."

I disconnected the call and went about putting my groceries away. I couldn't focus, and as hard as I tried, I couldn't think of a single thing I had done to warrant someone coming at me like this Bic monster.

I was sitting at my desk, trying and failing to write a paper for one of my professors, when a text came through from Simon.

Hey, I'm all done for the day, wanna get a bite?

I desperately needed the distraction.

Yes. I'll meet you at your dorm.

After cleaning up and changing, I made my way to Simon's, the whole time finding I was looking over my shoulder, hating the tendrils of fear that were nearly choking me. By the time I stepped foot into his building, it was as if I were taking a breath for the first time since leaving Greta Hall.

I knew I was doing a piss poor job of holding back my nervous expression when Simon's smiled faded as he opened the door.

"What's wrong?" He took my arm gently, ushering me inside.

"Nothing, why?"

He narrowed his eyes. "You're a horrible liar. What happened, was it that Fred person?"

I cocked my head. "How'd you know about Fred?"

"You told me."

I knew I'd shared with Simon that a guy had been bothering me, but I didn't recall giving him his name. I supposed I could've done so and forgotten, so I let it go.

"No, not Fred, I just got spooked is all."

Simon took a few steps, and then he was directly in front of me, cupping my face in his hands. His eyes intently searching my own. "What's going on, Rush?"

"You have your secrets, why can't I have mine?"

He sighed and closed his eyes briefly. "You want to keep this a secret, I won't push you. But I see it's bothering you, and I simply wanted to help." He released his hands from my face and the loss made my heart ache.

I didn't think Simon had the capacity to help me, but with my father not answering me and this huge asshole bothering me, maybe it would be a good idea to tell someone in case something happened to me.

"Okay, fine, you're right, something is bothering me."

Simon didn't say anything; he sat on the chair by his desk and waited patiently until I was ready to talk.

Unable to sit, I found myself pacing. "Yesterday I got a phone call. See, my father has a phone in my room only he calls me from…" I went on to tell Simon the whole story from the phone call, to speaking with my father, to the grocery store earlier today. Even gave him the guy's name, which to my surprise, Simon did not make a pen joke about.

When I was finished, it was like the adrenaline left my body and I felt wiped. With a *plop*, I sat on his bed and took a deep breath. I realized after a minute that Simon wasn't saying anything, and when I met his gaze there was an expression I'd never seen on his face before. He looked calculating, furious, ready to kill someone. It was fucking terrifying.

"Simon?"

He turned his head without saying a word and stared out the window. I knew he'd heard me, but there was this strange and scary cloud around him, as if he were figuring something out, and all I could do was sit and wait for him to speak.

I watched as he slid his cell phone out of his pocket and proceeded to call someone. What the hell was he doing?

"Simon! Are you—"

He held up a finger, indicating I should be quiet.

"Hey, I have a problem," he said to whomever he was talking to. "A big one." How did he have a problem when this was so clearly about me? "I don't know what you've been doing, but it's backfiring, and Rush is getting threats." *Wait a sec.*

I stood and walked over to Simon. He eyed me but didn't stop me.

"Some guy named Bic is threatening him. I think it's fair to say that whatever you all are doing there, it's not a secret to anyone over here."

I wanted to rip the phone away from his ear and ask who the fuck he was talking to, but I didn't.

"Yeah, maybe work faster." Simon looked up at me as I hovered above him. "In the meantime, I'm going to have to tell him everything, Snow. I don't have a choice anymore."

"Snow?"

Simon shook his head. "Talk to you later." He ended the call and slid his phone into his pocket.

"I think you're going to need to sit down, Rush. Because what I have to tell you will knock you on your ass."

I didn't take my eyes off Simon as I walked backward to the bed. When I felt the mattress hit my legs, I sat.

"Okay, I'm ready."

He huffed. "No, you're not."

CHAPTER FIFTEEN

Simon

Figuring out how to begin my story was the hardest part, but I knew when it was over, there was a good chance Rush would walk out that door and never return. I supposed it didn't matter how I started—the end would be the same, most likely.

"I'm about to tell you a lot of shit, Rush. You're not going to like most of it, and I understand you may never want to see me again afterward." He was about to interrupt, but I held up a finger. "Don't make a promise you don't know if you can keep by saying 'nothing I tell you will change how you feel,' because that's bullshit. What I will ask is only one thing. Let me tell the story to the end before you walk out of here."

"You're so sure I'll leave?"

I nodded. "Yeah."

Rush tightly fisted his hands together on his lap, readying himself, no doubt. "Okay, tell me."

"That guy who called you—Bic—I'm fairly sure he was referring to the snooping done by my family. Somehow, and I'm finding out how, your name got attached to it, and he thinks you're the one who is looking for answers."

"Answers on—"

"Let me talk, Rush. It's hard to get this all unjumbled."

"Okay."

"Remember the night in the Art Center when your father walked in?" Rush nodded. "I meant it when I said I should apologize to him, even if I didn't really think he deserved it. I wanted to make it easier on you and thought maybe if he liked me, it wouldn't be something he bothered you with."

Rush bit his lip; I was sure he wanted to interrupt me.

"So, I went over to the administrative building the next night after class. I had seen him go in while I was in the library and thought it was perfect. But when I got there, he wasn't alone."

Fuck. I did not want to tell him this part.

"Rush, your father is having a sexual relationship with that guy Fred who harasses you, and I saw it with my own two eyes. I didn't record them in the act, but I did take video of Fred leaving."

Rush's face was turning red, and I knew he was struggling not to explode, but he stared at me, listening.

"I heard what your father said to Fred about bothering you, and when you told me that was the guy, I wanted to tell you, but I thought it wasn't my place, because so what if your dad is with someone? But then I knew I wanted to tell you about me, who I was, everything. And when I talked to my pops and Snow, they said for everyone's protection they had to do background checks."

"I don't..." Rush started to speak but clamped up.

"I found out Fred's name, gave all the information to my family and have been waiting. But something we poked got someone's attention, and I think that's why that guy called you."

"Um, Simon...I'm...I'm going to process all this in a minute or ten, but I have to ask, why did your family need to do a background check?"

And this would likely be the clincher to him walking out.

"Right. Okay. My name is Simon, but my last name isn't Mancia."

"Shit," Rush whispered as he held his head in his hands. If he did that without knowing, I worried what he would think when he did, so I forged onward.

"My uncle's name is Christopher Manos. My name is Simon Manos. Not sure if you—"

He lifted his head face, eyes glistening with tears, but I wasn't sure what emotion he was feeling, maybe all of them.

"I know who the fuck Christopher Manos is. I know the stories of the biggest mobster in the world! I'm not some idiot." Anger. I could do anger.

"I know you're not an idiot, Rush."

"I don't know if I believe that. I…" He stood and was pacing again. "So this Bic guy found out who you were?"

"I don't think that's it, but I'm going to find out what's happening with this. I promise."

He stopped abruptly, his smile full of disdain. "Don't make a promise you don't know if you can keep, Simon." He shot my words back at me.

"Rush."

"No, please, just…" He took a few steps away from me. "I think I'm going to do that whole walking out of here thing now. I can't…I need to process all this."

I wanted to stop him more than anything, but I understood. I'd just thrown a ton of shit at him that was no doubt weighing him down. I hoped he would keep my secret about my name and while I should have told him not to tell a soul, instead I said, "Okay, Rush."

He nodded, turned with a jerk, and stormed out of my room. I wasn't sure I would ever see him again.

Rush hadn't reached out to me the whole week. I sent him a few texts telling him I was here if he needed me, but he never replied. I knew he had the AIDS charity open mic night this Saturday and hoped he was so busy that he was not thinking about how much he hated me.

All Snow and Pops could tell me was that they were close to figuring everything out and would let me know as soon as they had pieced it all together. I kept vigilant and was able to find out that while I hadn't seen Rush, he had not been harmed in any way.

Friday, after my last class, I trudged tiredly back to my dorm. I'd handed in three assignments and had two more to complete by next week. My brain was exhausted, my body was spent, and my heart…yeah, it ached.

The second I opened the door to my dorm room, I knew something wasn't right. It was as if the air were disturbed. I dropped my bag and shut the door. Moving to the corner, I took a moment to survey the whole room.

A squeak by the closet caught my attention. I reached into my pocket and took out my folded knife, ready.

When the closet door opened, the person who stepped out was not at all who I was expecting.

"It's been a long time since I came out of the closet." There, in all his glory, was Snow. A smile on his face, eyes as blue as the brightest sky, and…

"What on earth are you wearing?"

He looked down at himself. "A disguise." He tore off the long, dark wig and beige dress coat.

"Why were you in the closet?"

He rolled his eyes. "I'm going to pretend for a second you were raised with the Ingalls family on *Little House on the Prairie* and assume you don't realize that you literally can trust nothing and no one."

At that moment, while I had a million questions to ask, I was so happy to see him. Without warning, I flung myself at him, wrapping him in a huge hug. Through the years I had become taller and broader than Snow, but he and my pops were my protectors, and simply being near them turned me into that little eight-year-old boy who'd almost lost everything but instead had gained it all.

"Oh," Snow said, but soon he returned the hug and made no move to let go.

While we were still embracing, Snow decided to talk. "I wish I could say I was here to go shopping, but, my dear Eight, we have ourselves in a bit of a situation."

Reluctantly I pulled back. "How bad is this situation?"

He squished his nose and made a seesaw motion with his head. "Remember that time when the Sokolov family came after me and kidnapped me a few times and then I almost died like, what was it, twice…?"

"Twice? You have almost died like seven times. Don't pretend you don't know the exact number." I tapped his head.

"Fine…well, it's sort of like that. But probably worse."

Now I needed to sit. I went to my desk chair and fell into it.

"Worse, how?"

He smiled, the kind of smile like a parent was about to tell you that summer school was in your future.

"Like, oh wow, we went snooping around, and the Irish Mafia found out and, oh wait, Fred is the Irish kingpin's only son? Oh, wow…that bad."

"Shit."

"I was going to go with fuck, but okay, shit works." He leaned down and patted my shoulder.

"What does this mean?"

Snow shrugged like it was just another day. "I dunno, maybe a war, you may have to transfer out of here."

"War? Wait…what is Pops planning?"

This time Snow didn't smile. He looked me right in the eyes and said exactly what I knew he would.

"He's going to do whatever he has to, Eight."

CHAPTER SIXTEEN

Rush

"Everything looks amazing!" Luis said with a clap. "We will have an amazing event."

I wasn't feeling my jovial self, and I knew Luis could tell something was wrong, but I was relieved he didn't ask me.

"It always is." I patted Luis's shoulder. "I'm going to go backstage and get ready."

"Very good, yes, and I have to make sure the food is being prepared." He was off like a flash, and I went to the dressing room to get changed.

I was performing my first number with someone else. I would play piano, and Heather would be singing "Somewhere Over the Rainbow."

She was standing at the far end of the room, dressed in a red-sequined dress, her hair pinned up like a 1950s beauty, and ruby-red lips to match her gown. I would be wearing a standard tuxedo throughout my performances.

"Ready to sing?" I asked her as I sat in front of one of the mirrors.

"I've been practicing all week. I sing for so many things, but this event always makes me nervous." I looked in the mirror, and she stood behind me, smiling.

"You always knock 'em dead, Heather. I wouldn't worry."

"Thanks, Rush." She ruffled my hair—thankfully I hadn't combed it yet—and went over to talk to another one of the performers.

It was Open Mic Night, but too often people were afraid, and the first year Luis did this, no one sang, and he had no backup plan. So, there were a few of us who would be singing throughout the night to fill in what I was sure would be quiet moments.

Heather and I were opening it up tonight, and I made quick work of getting ready, knowing Luis would be opening the doors any minute.

"Welcome everyone," Luis's voice boomed happily through the speakers, and I got up and moved over to Heather. We would walk out together.

We listened as he explained about his late partner, the café, that all proceeds of Open Mic Night would go to the Jim Bastian Memorial Fund, and that even though there were some scheduled performers, anyone who wanted to participate could sign up by the bar.

"Now, it is my great pleasure to introduce to you, Rush and Heather, performing 'Somewhere Over the Rainbow.' "

I took Heather's hand, and together we walked on the stage. Lights shone brightly in my eyes and I couldn't see the crowd, but I heard the loud cheers. I took my seat in front of the piano while Heather thanked everyone and said she hoped to see many people taking the stage this evening. Then I began to play, and she sang so beautifully I almost wept.

After the song, Heather and I were thrilled to find out three people had signed up to perform. I went to the back to get into something a little more comfortable because I figured I could mingle a bit and maybe get more people up there and ask for donations.

"Hi, Rush." A few people from the university were there and I smiled and talked with them. So many had limited funds, but seeing that they came and had a drink and paid the cover charge was a nice thing.

A few times as I walked around the café, I didn't think about Simon. I thought that maybe I could do this. Then it happened; there he was, sitting at a small table…with someone. I couldn't tell who, except it was a woman. She wasn't facing me, and her hair was long and dark. She was saying something to Simon that had him laughing, and there was this adoration when he looked at her. A wave of jealousy crashed over me, and the next thing I knew my feet had taken me right over to his table.

"Simon," was all I said when I got there, and even I could hear the chill in my voice.

"Hi, Rush." He didn't shy away from meeting my gaze, but holding it was hard for me. I wanted to get lost in the way he looked at me. Instead, I decided to check out this woman who had Simon looking like he was on cloud nine.

She, on the other hand, would not look at me. She opted to sip her cosmopolitan.

"Excuse me, Miss, but may I ask your age?"

"Rush—"

I held my hand up cutting Simon off. "Simon here is underage, and…" I picked up his drink that appeared to be soda, but I was in full asshole mode, and sniffed it. "Glad to see there's no booze in there."

"I get that you're angry, Rush, but—"

"Miss, your age?"

She placed her drink down, and slowly peered up at me. Her eyes were the bluest I had ever seen…and the coldest. There was so little kindness to be seen, and the way she glared at me forced a shiver up my spine.

"That, sweet boy, is an extremely rude question to ask a patron. Do you not trust the bartenders who work here to make sure everyone who is given alcohol is properly vetted? Or do you get your kicks out of harassing people who come in for a night off and to contribute to a good cause?" Her voice was deeper than I assumed it would be, and upon closer inspection, I saw an Adam's apple.

I was the least judgmental person, but I was definitely curious about this woman who was with my...no, not my boyfriend. I didn't know what Simon and I were. But she was sharp-tongued and fierce.

"No, of course not, I...I'm sorry. You're right." I released a breath and took a careful look around, making sure we weren't on display. Fortunately, everyone was enthralled with the guy juggling and singing on stage.

"I know I'm right, and apology accepted." Her attention was off me and back on to Simon.

"Rush, we can go. I had promised I'd come to contribute, but I can see this is bothering you. We'll go."

But I didn't want that; I wanted him, them, to stay. "No, it's fine, really. I appreciate you being here. Let me buy you both a drink."

"Not much point in giving to a charity if you buy patrons drinks, now is it?" she said sarcastically.

"Hush," Simon snapped at her, which surprised me. She waved him off and sipped her drink some more.

"Miss, I am sorry for my rudeness. I'm Rush, I work here." I held out my hand, which she stared at for a moment before taking it. The shake was a jolt, and she narrowed her eyes at me.

"Mmmhmm, well, I said you were forgiven, but I don't forget, sweet boy." She winked then and turned to Simon. "I'm going to use the restroom."

I watched her go and took the vacated seat. "I didn't mean to be rude I...I saw you here and with her and—"

"Were you jealous?" He smiled, and I wanted to smack him.

"And my being jealous would make you happy?"

He shrugged, smile firmly in place. "Of course. That means you still kinda like me."

I huffed and glided my finger along the stem of the woman's glass. "Is it rude of me to ask who she is?"

When he burst out laughing, my lips curved. "It's funny how you think asking who she is comes off as rude, but you age-assaulted her a few minutes ago."

"I said sorry."

He took a sip of his soda. "She's from home. No one from here...family."

My eyes widened. Knowing now who his family was. "Your mom, sister?"

He lowered his voice, which forced me to lean in to hear. "My mom died when I was a baby. I never really knew her. Pops raised me. That lovely lady that you decided would become the victim of your bad mood? That's Snow, my pops's husband, and he has taken care of me since I was eight."

Snow Manos? Oh, for fuck's sake. I was going to die. Christopher Manos was going to find out I'd insulted the love of his life, and I'd be fitted with cement shoes and thrown in the ocean and never seen again.

"The panicked look on your face tells me you're likely thinking you'll be killed."

"Will I?" I swallowed, but it was like all the moisture left the room.

Simon chuckled. "No. You watch too many movies. Snow came by because of everything going on."

And it all fell like dominoes at that moment. Everything Simon had told me, and judging by his expression, he knew more. "Why would your family come here unless it was bad news?"

"They wouldn't, Rush. And I'm hoping after work you'll talk to me…or let me talk to you about what's going on." He didn't let me get a word in; he barreled onward. "I understand you probably don't want to see me anymore, but I at least need to tell you what's happening."

Every part of me wanted to tell him I did want to see him, that I wasn't so mad. But a stubborn part of me wanted him to stew.

"I won't be done until one."

"I'll take it!" he practically shouted, and before more could be said, Snow returned.

"First you take my dignity; now you take my chair."

I got up as fast as I could and held the chair out. "No, all yours, please, sit, don't be mad."

Simon laughed, and Snow looked at me as if I were crazy. I probably was, and as I met Simon's obsidian gaze from where I stood, I had a feeling things were about to get a lot more insane.

CHAPTER SEVENTEEN

Simon

Snow had left to go back to his hotel a little before midnight and made me promise to have the discussion with Rush there. He gave me a key card to get into his room and told me he wouldn't join the conversation unless I wanted him to.

A quarter after one in the morning, Rush came over to the end of the bar, where I was now sitting. He smiled awkwardly, the discomfort of our situation obvious.

"I'm ready," he said by way of greeting.

"Okay. We should talk somewhere private. I know I shouldn't ask this, but I need you to trust me a little here and come to a hotel with me."

His brows rose. "A hotel? Why not the dorms?"

"I can't risk anyone overhearing, and Snow has a room at a nearby hotel."

Rush looked over his shoulder, likely seeing if anyone was listening, but I'd been careful to make sure no one was close by.

"Fine."

"Thank you."

Rush was quiet as we walked to my car, not arguing that he had to leave his behind. He got into the passenger seat, belted up, and proceeded to stare out the window the entire drive to the hotel.

We pulled up to the Kentmore Hotel, ridiculously fancy but no question—my pops would not let Snow stay anywhere less than fabulous.

"Nice hotel," Rush muttered, getting out of the car. I handed the key to the valet and went over to Rush.

"Leave it to my family to find the nicest place in town." I tried to lighten the mood, but Rush had this dark cloud surrounding him. I couldn't tell if it was fear over the situation, anger at me—I had no idea. But regardless of what happened to the two of us, I'd put his life in danger…well, my entire family, actually, so we needed to fix it.

"Good evening, sir," the doorman said.

"Evening."

We walked in, and the opulence was almost overbearing. Out of the corner of my eye I saw Rush looking up and around, taking it all in. I just wanted to get up to the room and get this talk over with. I went to the elevators and hit the up arrow.

"Is your uncle here?" Rush asked as we stood, waiting for the elevator.

"No."

"Hmm."

I peered over at him, his face wrinkled in confusion.

"Why hmm?"

Shrugging, he answered, "From what I can gather about the, um, Mafia, no one goes anywhere alone." He whispered, thankfully, but his "hmm" was making more sense.

"True…I mean, I came here by myself."

"Under the guise of being someone else."

The elevator doors opened, and we went inside. I pressed the button and waited until we were ensconced within to speak.

"I can't imagine my pops letting Snow come here, knowing there's a serious issue, unprotected."

"Unless he snuck here."

No, that wasn't how things worked. "Nah."

The doors opened and the question of whether Snow had come here alone was answered.

"Well, well, well, not-so-small fry. College life is treating you well." Mace stood in front of the elevator, blocking our path. He was one of my pops's guys and stupidly in love with Bill, another of Pops's guys. Speaking of Bill…

"Mace, move the fuck out of the way so they can get out of the elevator." He gripped Mace's shoulder and pulled him back.

Yeah, they had a special kind of love. They'd started out truly hating each other. Mace had worked for an assassin organization and Bill had worked for Pops. They'd been teamed up together to stop some shithead hell-bent on taking over Haven Hart and killing Snow. After working together and Mace nearly getting killed, they realized their hate had actually turned into love. Mace had lost a finger and had a scar across his forehead from being tortured, but it didn't seem to bother him. Pops had felt responsible and asked Mace to work with him. For years these two guarded my family and seeing them, even under these horrible circumstances, was really nice.

"Hi, Mace, Bill." I gestured over to Rush. "This is Rush."

"Ah, you're Rush." Mace smiled as if he were preparing to tease. I knew Rush was on edge, so I walked off the elevator and he followed.

"I have a key card, no need to help."

"Yeah, Snow told us, but Mace was like a kid and wanted to see you. You tell Snow if he sneaks out of that hotel room again without one of us with him, I will call Christopher."

Ahh, so that explained how the two times I'd seen Snow yesterday and today, neither Bill nor Mace had been with him. I wondered why Snow hadn't told me they were here.

"I will." I slipped the key card in and opened the door.

It was quiet and the lights were dimmed, so I assumed Snow was in the bedroom. I walked deeper into the hotel room and over to the sitting area. It wasn't a gigantic room, but it was big enough. From the window I could see Abernathy University, and I knew I had to talk to Rush.

"Have a seat, want a drink?"

"No, I'm fine." He sat on the chair, his gaze moving all over the room, taking it in.

"What can you tell me about Fred Brennan?" I sat across from him and cut right to the chase.

"He's an annoying little shit. I once thought his nose was so far up my father's ass because he wanted to be like him, I now see that they are...I can't say it."

"So, you believe me about that?"

He met my eyes and nodded. "I didn't like anything you said to me, Simon, but I didn't say I never believed you."

"Thanks, Rush." The relief of hearing him say that had me taking a very audible breath.

"Simon, I won't lie, I'm mad. You had no right to do a lot of what you did without talking to me. You were fine keeping secrets of your own and calling the shots, and I didn't push you. But you taking it upon yourself to poke through my life...my dad's? I don't give a fuck about Fred, but it's still an invasion."

"I know, you're right."

"I don't need your validation, Simon!" His voice rose, he stood, but he collected himself and sat back down.

"Sorry."

"I shouldn't yell, I'm sure your...is it dad, is sleeping."

"You can call him my dad, I do sometimes. I just knew him as

Snow first, like he knew me as Eight. It's what we call each other, but he's a dad in every sense of the word."

Rush folded his hands on his lap and was focused on staring at the carpet. "About Fred. I don't know a whole lot. He's an asshole to me, though he has left me alone, and I don't know if it's thanks to my dad or you or—"

"I nor anyone in my family has spoken to anyone. My guess is Fred is listening to your father."

"Something my father did right," Rush mumbled, and I felt like he was saying that more to himself than to me, so I ignored it.

"But here's the problem, Rush."

Now he did look at me, and I wished he wouldn't, because this was going to suck.

"Fred is the son of the head of the Irish Mafia in this area. Bic works for Fred's father, and when we went digging we hit a land mine, so to speak."

Rush covered his face with his hands and slowly slid them down. "How much worse are you going to make this?"

"I never intended...look, hate me, fine, but did you think the Irish weren't going to find out that the boss's only son was fucking the prestigious Rushmore Abernathy the Second? They would have. And I don't know if they do know yet. Honestly, I have no idea what they understand about Fred. But I can imagine it would be hell for your father if it came to light."

Rush stood and began pacing in front of the window. "Maybe my father knows already. Don't you think Fred would tell him?"

"I think if your father knew that and was continuing a sexual relationship with him, your father is extremely foolish."

Rush froze, staring at me through narrowed eyes. "Or Fred is playing my father! This is on Fred's shoulders. He has answering to do."

He and I were in agreement on that for sure. "I don't disagree, but we can't just grab him and throw him in front of us to answer questions. We do that and we show our hand, and we are in the wrong."

"But if we don't do something, my father could die."

The door to the bedroom opened and Snow walked out, empty glass in hand and heading to the kitchen area. He quirked a brow at us as if to say this drama was interfering with his sleep.

"I don't mean to interrupt, just getting water. Carry on with your theories." He opened the small fridge and took out a bottle. We both watched as he poured the water into the glass.

"Theories?" Rush asked.

"Mmm. A hypothesis assumed for the sake of argument or investigation. An unproved assumption, conjecture. Abstract thought, speculation. That's a theory, college boy."

"I...um." Rush looked at me, but I rolled my eyes.

"Ignore him, Rush, he's a show-off."

"Pardon?" Snow brought a hand to his chest. "That's rude." He sipped his water, his blue eyes darting between the two of us. "Okay, I'm gonna say something."

"Of course you are." I sighed and sat back. There was no stopping him.

"Rush, your father may die. I won't sugarcoat it for you. But let's be real for a minute. Nothing Eight, I, or my side of things do is going to be the reason for it. Your dad is having relations with the Irish kingpin's son. And from what I know about Liam Brennan, he isn't tolerant of homosexuals."

"Liam Brennan?" Rush seemed to disregard the whole part about his father dying and went straight to asking about Fred's dad.

"Yes indeed, that's who is in charge in these parts."

"And he's dangerous?"

"Oh, you sweet summer child." Snow tsked and walked over to Rush. "Yes, as dangerous as the men outside this room, the one who holds my heart, and the one who is staring at you like you hung the moon."

Rush looked over at me, and I shrugged. "You are kinda amazing."

Rush shook his head. "Can we stay on one conversation?"

"I'm going to sleep. You two keep at it but, Eight, Christopher isn't going to be okay with you walking anywhere unprotected."

I'd known that was coming. "And Bill told me to tell you if you sneak out of here without one of them again, he'll call Pops."

Snow huffed. "Snitches."

"What do I do?" Rush sounded so helpless.

"My advice?" Snow brought his glass back to the kitchen. "Do what I did many years ago."

"And what's that?" Rush watched as Snow started to walk to the bedroom.

"Trust the man who would die for you."

CHAPTER EIGHTEEN

Rush

As soon as Snow was in the other room, the door was shut, and I felt as if Simon and I had some semblance of privacy, I turned to him, no doubt shock showing on my face. "You'd die for me?"

He leaned forward, and even though he was sitting and I was standing, it felt like Simon was the bigger man.

"When I first saw you only two weeks ago, singing on that stage on the green, I knew you had something. I wasn't sure at first what it was, so I went and saw you perform at The Falsetto Café. Talking to you was the easiest thing I'd ever done. And it was the first time I truly regretted living this lie about who I was. I had never asked my pops if I could bring someone in, to let them know who I was. It's so dangerous that you do, Rush, and I didn't lie because I thought I was better than anyone. And I never meant to find anything out about your dad like I did."

He sighed and stood up but did not move. "I won't apologize that my family did what they did to keep me safe, but I do apologize for the shit it's causing. But, Rush, this thing with Fred and your dad…it can't end well."

I knew he was right and sincere. I understood why his family had done the poking around, and maybe I was jealous over how much his family loved him, that they would go through so much trouble. It had taken my father argument after argument just for him to get Fred to leave me alone. And he'd been fucking the guy the whole time.

"I admit, I don't know your life. What it's like. I read the stories, watch the news and stuff, but it's media based, and I'm sure they don't even show the tip of the iceberg when it comes to what your life is really like." I took a step closer to Simon, an invitation for him to move too.

"A lot of the media think they know, and it's fair to say they are led to believe certain facts that do get out." He smirked as if he felt no shame in that. He inched toward me. "You need to talk to your dad, Rush."

He was right, and yet a small part of me wanted to let him deal with his impending doom on his own. No, he was the only family I had left. "What do I tell him?"

"You can start by asking him about his relationship with Fred."

I could just see how well that would go. "He would get seriously defensive; then he'd want to know how I found out. Me telling him the Manos family informed me wouldn't have positive results."

"Well, him fucking the son of Liam Brennan, head of the Irish Mafia, won't either."

I flinched, unable to hide my reaction. "Let me talk to my dad my way. I…there's no way to say this in a respectful way."

"I could go with you." Simon stood directly in front of me now, and I could not remember him coming closer.

"That would be worse."

"You can't be alone. This Bic guy has it out for you, and until my pops has figured out how to keep them away from you—"

"Are you about to tell me I can't go anywhere alone?"

The silence that followed was not reassuring.

"Simon, how am I going to explain someone shadowing me everywhere I go?"

"They won't know. Mace and Bill are really good at what they do, and I have a sneaking feeling one of them is here to watch over you."

My gaze went directly toward the door. "So when I walk out of here, one will follow?"

Simon gently touched my shoulder. "I think we should stay here tonight. It's almost two in the morning. Tomorrow is Sunday...Well, technically today is Sunday. Will you stay, and we can talk about this over breakfast?"

"Where exactly do you expect me to sleep?"

He hooked a thumb over his shoulder. "There's a spare bedroom."

Looking over at the couch, there was no way Simon could sleep there without getting one hell of a crick in his neck. "Double beds?"

He shook his head. "I'll stay out here, I don't—"

"No, it's fine. I don't want your dad coming out and seeing you sleeping on the couch. He'll likely jump on my sleeping form and scratch my eyes out."

Simon smirked. "He would not! But I promise to be a gentleman. I don't really want to sleep on the couch."

"Who would? Come on." I headed toward the bedroom with Simon close behind me.

I was enveloped in the most wonderful warmth. The sun was up and dimly shining on my face, strong fuzzy arms hugged me and…*Wait a second!* I jolted upright, making Simon grunt.

"What?" he said; then his eyes widened, and he jumped out of bed, on the defensive. "What is it?"

"You!" I realized he had a small tissue box in his hand. "Were you going to attack someone with that?"

"Huh?" He looked at the box and quickly dropped it. "I grabbed what I could, you were freaked out, so I thought someone was in here."

"Well, thank God you'll have some two-ply when I die."

He cocked his head, showing that sexy morning smirk, and bedroom eyes. "You're adorable when you rhyme in the morning."

"Uh-huh, okay, so, breakfast?" I figured I'd move past the whole Simon jumping out of bed like he was on fire part.

"It's…" He checked the time on his phone. "Wow, it's almost eleven."

"I'm starving." I grabbed my pants, since I'd slept in my shirt and boxers, and went toward the bathroom.

"Why'd you jump out of bed?"

Shit. "Oh, um…I was confused, forgot where I was." Totally playing it off because I wasn't sure I was ready for him to know that when he was close, touching me, wrapping me up in those strong arms, I felt safe and loved. No, he couldn't know that, and I was having trouble accepting it.

Flickers of emotion flashed across Simon's face. I had a feeling he wasn't buying it, and I was readying myself for an argument, but he just gave a nod and moved to grab his own clothes.

I went into the bathroom and shut the door, resting my forehead on the cool wood. This entire situation was a clusterfuck of epic proportions, and I both wanted to work things out with

Simon and also say fuck this and fuck you, I'm out. But I couldn't find my way.

After I cleaned up and thankfully, brushed my teeth—gotta love luxury hotels—I went out to the bedroom to find it empty. I followed the sound of voices to the seating area where we were at last night. There I saw Simon sitting in a chair and Snow on the couch next to the big guy with short blond hair and a beard that made him kind of look like a Viking. And sitting on the arm of the couch was the man who'd greeted us at the elevator. I forgot their names.

"There you are, all nice and clean?" Snow seemed to have this way of making you question if he was honestly asking you something or being sarcastic. I took my chances.

"Yeah, thanks."

"Lovely. I heard you were starving, so I took the pleasure of ordering a few things. It will be here soon, sit, sit."

I looked and didn't see another seat, so I grabbed a stool from by the breakfast bar and sat on it.

"We have a lot to talk about, it would seem." Snow had one leg draped over his other, a coffee cup he was sipping almost daintily, and I found myself entranced by his eyes. "Hello, anyone home?"

"What, sorry, it's just. Is it rude to ask how old you are? Because I mean, you don't look much older than us."

One side of Snow's mouth curled up and he looked over at the Viking and fluttered his lashes. "Hear that, Bill? I look like a youngun'."

Bill rolled his eyes and grumbled something inaudible. This made the other guy hit him on the back of the head.

"Fuck, Mace, quit it." Bill pushed Mace, and he almost fell off the couch.

"Children, behave." Snow placed his cup down and smiled

brightly at me. "I'd much rather pretend to be the age you think I am."

"Sorry." I looked at Simon, who appeared to be trying to hold in a bout of laughter.

"Oh, do not be sorry." Snow chuckled. "Now, as much as I'd love for you to tell me I look fabulous, we do need to discuss how we go forward and what we're going to do about getting you off the Brennan family's radar."

"Maybe I could talk to my dad, see what he knows? Simon suggested it last night." It felt like I was swallowing sand. These men, minus Simon, made me nervous. I looked over at the one with the longish dark hair, Mace. He was chewing gum and would smile whenever I made eye contact. He seemed nice but he was a murderer, I knew it. Same with Bill. Snow, I wasn't sure of. Wait, was Simon?

"You absolutely need to speak with Daddy Dearest." Snow laughed. "And we think it best we be present."

"I'm sorry, are you crazy?" I jumped off the stool. "This is personal. If I drag you all there to—"

"No, you can bring him here, it's safer," Snow said.

"How do I do that? Have you met my father? The only time I speak to him is to argue with him about my life. It's hostile and unwelcome."

You could have heard a pin drop after my outburst. I hadn't meant to say that, but it had erupted from within me. And what hurt my heart even more was the truth of my statement. My father was distant, and I thought he loved me, but it was sad that I questioned it.

"Oh, sweet boy." And then there were arms around me, and I had a face full of white hair. "Let it all out."

"I'm not crying." I had my arms at my side while Snow's were like a vise around me.

"It's going to be okay."

"I am okay." I looked over at Simon, who was no longer trying not to laugh.

"You're better than okay." Snow pulled back and cradled my face in his hands. "I won't let anyone hurt you, I promise. If they try, they will die the most painful death."

"Death by papercuts?" Mace asked gleefully.

"Sure, dear." Bill pushed Mace again, this time making him fall off the couch.

"Don't kill my father," I pleaded.

Snow smiled softly, like an angel, but his words were that of the devil. "Then he'd better not hurt you anymore."

CHAPTER NINETEEN

Simon

With Mace shadowing us, Rush and I returned to campus. Regardless of anything, Rush and I did have classes, and he wanted to phone his dad and ask him to join him for lunch the following day to talk. Snow had agreed to meet Rush halfway and reserved a private room in a nearby restaurant. The one thing he would not budge on was Rush speaking to his father alone.

Rush was pretty sure that by the time his father realized what was going on, it wouldn't matter who was there. I figured part of Rush hoped his dad would be mortified by the discovery of his scandalous relationship. I didn't know the eldest Abernathy enough to know if that was the case.

"We can go to your dorm first," Rush said as we got out of my car. Mace had driven Rush's car back from the café to the campus at some point this morning, which I was grateful for.

"First?"

"Well, I figured you're not going to let me be alone, and Mace isn't going to be able to watch you and me, so…"

He did not finish, so I had to guess where he was going with this. "You want me to stay with you in your dorm?"

We were walking toward my building when he stopped suddenly. "I don't know how this all works, Simon. I know I like you and that I'm still a little peeved at you. But I'm also afraid, and I'm not too proud to admit that. This is the Irish Mafia we're dealing with, and that guy Bic found out a private number and tracked me down in the supermarket." He sighed, looking around as if someone were going to jump out at him.

"Yeah, okay, I don't mind staying with you. And right now, your safety is most important. Us, you and me, we'll figure that out."

There was longing and frustration in his eyes, and I knew the biggest battle Rush was facing at that moment was with himself.

"Sounds good." He started walking again and I followed behind. I couldn't see Mace, but I knew he was there.

I packed a small duffle, enough for a few days, and watched as Rush meandered around my room, looking over things. I wondered if it made sense to him now that I had so few personal items here. I also wondered if he'd thought about how I'd told him I would be following in my pops's footsteps with his business and if he truly understood what that meant.

"When is your first class tomorrow?" he asked, pulling me from my thoughts.

"Nine, you?"

"Same. I don't have anything after one, so lunch will be at one thirty, right?"

We went over the time for lunch tomorrow, and the only worry was hoping Rush's father wouldn't give him a hard time. The fact that he was repeating stuff he already knew proved how nervous he was.

"Yeah, just hope it works for your dad."

He scoffed. "I'll make it enticing enough for him to be sure not to miss it."

I was curious about what he would say, but I also knew I would be in the dorm room when he called, so I would find out soon enough.

When I'd gathered everything I needed, we left and walked toward Greta, where we planned on staying the rest of the day. Maybe I could convince Rush to order pizza, and we could watch a movie so he would be able to clear his head.

The sun was setting as we entered Greta Hall, and exhaustion was present in every step Rush and I took. We had not slept well the night before with everything going on, and we were exhausted.

"Here we are." He opened the door, and the first thing we saw was the red light blinking on his answering machine. Yes, he had an answering machine that was attached to the phone his father gave him. He went over and hit the button while I shut and locked the door.

"*Rushmore, it's your father, call me as soon as you get this.*" That was the first message.

"Well, it will make a reason for calling him easier," Rush said, and then the next message played.

"*Hello, we have been trying to reach you about your car's extended warranty—*" Rush hit delete.

"God, those robocalls are everywhere." I laughed and plopped on the small couch.

"*Rush, it's Bic, I felt we had an understanding, I'm beginning to think you're slow or somethin'. Last warning.*"

"*End of new messages.*" The auto-voice spoke, and Rush and I looked at each other.

"You call your dad; I'll call Snow." I got up and stepped just outside the room so we would both have privacy.

I called Snow, and he picked up on the second ring. "What's up, buttercup?" he said by way of greeting.

"Hey, so that guy Bic called."

"Stop or else? Was it something like that?"

"Yeah."

"Okay, let me call Christopher and see where he's at with all this. You two sit tight. Maybe stay inside."

"For the night, yes. Rush is talking to his dad too, and we have class in the morning."

Snow sighed. "Very well, but be safe."

"I want Mace to stay with Rush tomorrow. He's the target in all this."

I sensed Snow wanted to argue, but he had a lot of respect for me and my choices.

"Okay, Eight."

"I'll text you once I hear what Rush's dad says."

"I appreciate that. Sleep well."

We disconnected, and I went back into the room to find Rush lying on his bed with his arm draped over his eyes.

"What's wrong?"

"My father has been suspended, pending an investigation."

I took the two steps to Rush's bed and sat on the edge. "For Fred or—"

"All he explained to me was that he was presented with a letter from the board saying he was suspended effective immediately, pending an investigation of immoral conduct."

"Immoral conduct? Is that a thing here?"

Rush nodded and slid his arm off his face. "I told him to meet me for lunch so we could talk, and I don't know if he was just defeated or what, but he gave me no argument when I told him when and where."

"We'll find out everything."

He sat up, eyes squinted. "Did Snow or your dad or whoever

is poking into my life make this happen to my father?"

I chuckled, but I could tell from the expression on Rush's face that he did not appreciate it. "Sorry, no, that's not how my family works."

"How'd they find out then? Because Fred is the only reason I could think of as to why this is happening." I knew Rush didn't want to think badly of his father. He was all there was left in his family, so I tried to be understanding when I answered.

"Rush, I stumbled upon your dad and Fred; is it too farfetched to think someone else stumbled too?"

Rush's whole body deflated. "No, I suppose not. It just feels so coincidental."

"It does, I agree. That's why I said we would figure it out."

The sun was practically set and with no illumination in his room, it felt unsettling. I got up and clicked on the tall light he had in the corner, bathing the room in a warm glow.

"Let's order pizza and watch horrible movies." Offering him a smile, I was relieved when he smirked.

"Sure, why not? Nothing else we could do tonight."

Oh, no there was a lot we could do tonight, but Rush was unsure about us, and I was not about to fuck up my chance to be with him again by making a move too soon.

"Great. You pick the movie, I'll order pizza."

He sat up fast. "Wait. This is serious."

It did not sound serious, so I cocked my head and waited for him to explain.

"How do you know what I like on my pizza?"

"Hmm." I tapped my chin comically. "Wanna see if I have you figured out in the ways of pizza?"

He pursed his lips, eyes squinted for a moment. "Okay, let's see if you know my pizza preferences, and I'll see if I know your movie ones."

Oh, this was going to be good.

CHAPTER TWENTY

Rush

Simon had ordered a meat lover's pizza, which was exactly what I would have chosen, and I'd picked the first movie in the Avengers franchise, knowing they were his favorite from a conversation we'd had. He said this was one of his favorites in the series and that we could do a crappy movie night another time, and I found that I loved thinking there would be more nights with him.

The internal struggle over whether being with Simon was a good idea or not was easily being decided on its own with every sweet thing he did.

We ate pizza on the small couch, talked about our classes, and when it came time to watch the movie, I encouraged him to lie on the bed since it would be easier to watch it off my laptop that way.

We got about halfway through before we both passed out. Not surprising with all we had been through mentally the last twenty-four hours.

I jolted awake when I heard loud laughter in the corridor and turned to see Simon, one hand behind his head, the other resting on my thigh. He was sleeping, his glasses askew on his face.

I watched him for a few moments, the happy sounds outside beginning to fade. And like a magnet to metal, I moved closer to him and tenderly pressed a kiss to his lips.

When I pulled away, his dark endless gaze was staring at me. I didn't wait for him to speak or for either of us to question what I was doing. I kissed him again. He returned it, softly, tentatively as if wondering if what was happening was real, and a small part of me wondered that too.

I became lost in our kiss, only realizing Simon was moving the laptop onto the floor when I heard a slight *thud*. Then I was wrapped in his arms, lying atop his body, ravishing his mouth as need consumed me.

Through our jeans I could feel how hard he was, and I moaned into the kiss as our cocks pressed against each other. Not one word was spoken, as if this moment were so fragile only feelings were allowed here.

I slid along his body, rubbing my cheeks over his chest, and even though he still had his shirt on, it was his smell of fresh pine and vanilla. I didn't know if it was his body wash or natural scent, but I was becoming addicted to it.

The feel of him stroking my hair urged me further until I was mouthing his denim-clad erection. I wanted him in my mouth, needed it like air. I made quick work of unbuttoning and unzipping his jeans and pulling them down with his briefs, allowing his cock to spring free.

He watched me through hooded eyes, his gaze making me feel like I hung the moon, and damn, I wanted to make him fly. I swiped my tongue on the underside of his cock and swirled around the tip, enjoying when he hissed.

When my tongue was coated with his precome, I swallowed, loving his taste, he fisted my hair and fuck, I welcomed the pain.

With my free hand I opened my pants, releasing my cock and jacking it in time with my sucking. He bucked up into my mouth, fucking it as I increased my ministrations on my cock. I was chasing my orgasm as much as I was wanting his.

The second the bitter yet sweet splash of his come hit my tongue, I came in my fist. Every drop he gave me felt like ecstasy, and when he relaxed, his breathing heavy, I slipped his cock from my mouth and smiled at him.

"Rush, I—"

"No, please, no words."

I rested my head on his thigh, and for however many minutes I lay there, I pretended this world only consisted of Simon and me and none of the crap outside these walls.

As promised, Simon did not talk about what happened, but everything around the two of us felt lighter as we got ready for classes that morning. Our first classes were close by, so we walked together, splitting off when he went into one building and I into another. We had agreed to go to the restaurant together for lunch and for me to meet him by his car.

I half listened to my professors as they spoke, but I didn't worry because catching up was never hard for me. I'd never had love for these subjects and was doing all of this for my father anyway.

I was early meeting Simon at his car and soon saw I wasn't alone.

"He won't be here for, like, another twenty minutes." Mace leaned against the Benz, arms folded, eyes watching everywhere.

"Yeah, I know." I had a million questions for this man beside me but was terrified to ask them.

"It's kinda weird seeing Simon in a relationship."

I looked over at him, thinking that couldn't be true. "He said he's had boyfriends and girlfriends."

Mace shrugged. "I mean, he was seeing someone right before he left, but they were kids in a sense, and it was more like they were just friends. And since he's been at college, he's never let any of us meet anyone."

"Keeping his life as secretive as he has, it would be difficult to do that, don't you think?"

Mace was watching a couple of guys playing frisbee on the green as he spoke. "I dunno. I don't think Simon ever thought he'd meet anyone in college. He wanted his education, then to move home and take his place."

"His place?"

He turned toward me, more serious than I had ever seen him. "He's the heir, so to speak, of the Manos family. As much as Christopher didn't want this life for Simon, Simon wants it, and Christopher will teach him."

Realizing that when Simon had told me he was majoring in business to help his family—that meant the mob. Staying with Simon meant being in that life.

"Right."

Mace nudged me with his shoulder. "I'm gonna say something; you do with it as you will, okay?"

I nodded, unable to speak as everything felt like an assault on my whole future.

"If you decide to go down this path with Simon, you need to realize what it is and accept it. You have to maybe love him even if you don't love the job. I've been in this life since I could breathe, so I don't really understand anything else. But people like Snow, they learned to love the man and in doing so realized he would do anything for them. You need to reconcile that fact, or when this is all done with your father, let Simon go."

I knew he was right. A choice had to be made.

"I can see you mean a lot to him already, and I worry about the little guy...well, not so little, but you get me."

"Yeah. I don't mean to or want to string him along."

Mace smiled, and it made the already pretty man even more gorgeous. The scar across his forehead made the flawlessness more real. "I know, he knows too."

Just then I saw Simon walking toward us from across the green. His eyes moving all around, ever vigilant. I wondered if he realized people moved out of the way for him when he walked. It was his presence, and it exhibited power. Clearly, though, he was oblivious.

"Hey." He smiled at both of us. "Ready to eat?"

"I feel like throwing up."

He chuckled at me. "You're not alone in this, Rush, promise. We got you."

And as I got in his car and drove to the restaurant with him, I felt that to be true. I was safe with him, and knowing that some of Simon's family would be there with me, even though they didn't have to be, meant more to me than I would admit.

CHAPTER TWENTY-ONE

Simon

The restaurant Snow chose was perfect. There was a dining area, but in the back was a spacious private room. Snow had asked for everyone to be seated at a large round table since it was easier to converse that way.

I walked in with Rush and Mace and saw the round table and three servers standing by the wall, likely waiting for the whole party to arrive. Snow and Bill were clearly talking about something light—Snow was laughing and Bill rolled his eyes.

"There you all are." Snow came over and hugged me as if he hadn't seen me in years. "Rush, are you meeting your father in the front of the restaurant and bringing him here?"

"Yeah, I figured that would be best."

Snow gave him a nod. "Okay, well, he should be here soon. Why don't you go now? But stay inside. No need to expose yourself." Snow looked at Mace. "Maybe go with him—extra eyes."

"Is that really nece—"

Rush was interrupted by Snow. "All of it is necessary, trust me."

Rush didn't argue, and I watched him and Mace leave the room. "This isn't going to be an easy day for him, Snow."

"No, Eight, it's not. But sometimes we need to do things and say things that hurt, and we spend far too much time healing afterward."

All I could do was agree with him. There was not much else I could do. The things my family and I had been through, typical people had not, and while Rush had lived a less than stellar childhood, it wasn't nightmare inducing.

Snow went over to the table and sat, Bill next to him. We had discussed that Rush should not be directly next to his father, so Rush would sit next to Bill, and I would be on his other side followed by Mace and then Rush's dad…putting his father right next to Snow.

I knew Bill hated that, but there was no talking Snow out of it. Snow wanted to be close to the senior Abernathy for reasons that were his own.

I was going to wait to sit so I could guide people to where they were sitting. Rush knew to sit beside Bill, but nothing more. So he would walk in and go directly there.

Soon enough the door opened, and Rush stepped in. The clear nervousness of his demeanor made me want to hug him and promise him I would fix all this, but I stayed put, and he went right to his seat.

"What's all this, Rushmore?" His father's eyes were wide and wild as he took in the room and the people he had not been expecting.

Mace came in last, shutting the door. Rush's father turned and stepped away, probably because Mace had a pretty menacing smile going on.

"Father, we need to talk. It's got to do with why you're suspended and well, just sit, please." Rush sat and I quickly took my own seat. Mace, ever the gentleman, went over to where dear old dad was to sit and pulled out his chair.

"Who are these people?"

"Mr. Abernathy, my name is Snow Manos; I'm one of Simon's fathers." Snow smiled brightly, and even though we were in the midst of an uncomfortable moment, hearing Snow say that warmed me.

"Manos…" Rush's father's expression went from annoyed to terrified.

"Have a seat, sir." Mace gestured to where he was to sit and when he took it and we were all ready, Snow began.

"Your son hasn't lied to you, if you're wondering. The two of you desperately need to have a heart-to-heart, but what I'm here to tell you is that the choices you have made have greatly affected his life and dangerously impacted my family."

"What? Rushmore, what is he talking about, and how did you get messed up with mobsters?"

"Mr. Abernathy." Snow spoke louder to get his attention. "I would like to offer you one warning. Do not disrespect my family by making mine seem beneath yours. Trust me when I tell you the Manos family always rises above."

Rush's dad looked chagrined, and I was glad to see he was being put in his place. I did not like him, but he was the father of the man I cared about, so I would do my best to hold back from telling him to go fuck himself.

"My apologies, Mr. Manos."

Snow signaled to the servers, and they made quick work of getting everyone's drink orders. I had no doubt these servers were paid a ridiculous amount of money for their silence. I also would not be shocked if they actually worked for my pops to begin with.

"Now, shall we have a somewhat civilized conversation?" Snow smiled.

"Please." Rush's dad gulped down his water, showing us just how nervous he was.

Snow glanced at me, and I knew I was up. "Mr. Abernathy." Both Rush and his dad looked over at me. I knew Rush hadn't known I would be speaking—he was under the assumption Snow or he would. But this part had to be me. I never shied away from things that landed on my shoulders.

"I won't address why I lied about who I was to you, because I'm sure you can understand why anonymity, for me, is so important."

He nodded, eyes flickering toward Snow, Bill, and Mace.

"When we first met, it didn't go well, and I wanted to make amends, mostly for Rush's sake. So, one night I went to your office. It was there I found you with Fred."

"You're the one who reported me?" He slammed his hands on the table, the silverware clanging and the crystal glasses clinking. Mace placed a hand on his shoulder and firmly pushed his back against his chair.

"Control yourself." Then Mace removed his grip.

"If you'll let me finish, Mr. Abernathy, you will get the whole story."

I went on to explain to him everything from the very beginning. I apologized for my part and my family's part for bringing awareness to the poking around.

"I don't understand." Mr. Abernathy appeared confused. "How does your family poking into our backgrounds alert the school board? I should think you're all well-versed in stealthy snooping."

This was where Snow came in. "We were as stunned as you were to see what our everyday digging had found. Fred, the man you're involved with and the likely reason you were suspended, is the son of Irish Kingpin Liam Brennan."

"What!" Judging by how surprised he was, Fred had never shared that with him.

"If I had to guess, I'd say Daddy Brennan knew about you and his son, or found out fairly recently, and he would be the reason you're under investigation." Bill quirked a brow.

"But if you all hadn't poked around, he never would have found out," he argued.

"Father." Rush spoke for the first time. "Regardless of how the board found out, you broke the rules. Rules you…our family…put in place. If they don't hold you responsible for what you've done—"

"Responsible for what I've done?" He narrowed his eyes at his son. "I care greatly for Fred."

"Do you, Mr. Abernathy? And how does he feel about you?" Snow asked. "I hope your answer is a whole hell of a lot because Fred's homosexuality will get him killed. In the eyes of his father, Fred is abhorrent. Do you care enough about him to stand between father and son?"

No one spoke; all that could be heard were the servers milling around setting up the salads. The fact that Rush's father did not answer right away told me more than I needed to know. The thing was, I would absolutely stand between Rush and his dad, and I would answer in under a second.

"And it's that silence, Mr. Abernathy, that will not only kill Fred and you, but it will kill your son." Snow cocked his head. "Did your son's well-being ever even cross your mind?"

"Snow," Rush hurried to interrupt. "It doesn't matter about that right now, just our safety and how we don't piss off Liam Brennan any more than we clearly have."

"You say 'we.' " Mace turned to Rush. "Yeah, we looked into Fred's background, but your father was fucking him. Never mind that he was doing it understanding he was breaking policy, but the way I see it is, we can throw Dad and Fred to the Brennans and call it a day."

"Is that what you'd like, Rush?"

This part we'd sort of rehearsed, much to Rush's dislike. "No, I don't want anyone to die."

Mace scoffed, and Bill rolled his eyes.

Snow gave Rush's dad a smile. "Will you work with us, Mr. Abernathy, and hopefully save both your lives?"

"What about Fred?" It was as if Fred's life were more important than his son's, and I could feel the hurt pang through Rush.

"Hmm...And if it meant we save Fred and your son dies, then what, Mr. Abernathy?"

Rush's dad looked at Rush and back to Snow. "Why does anyone have to die?"

Snow sighed, hands clasped in front of him. "In these situations, Mr. Abernathy, someone always dies. Question you need to ask yourself is, where do your loyalties lie?"

Waiting for Rush's father to respond was painful, and I watched as Rush's entire face crumbled. Though he sat in silence, he knew. He did not mean as much to his father as he'd thought. That alone made me want to jump across the table and strangle the life out of the man.

"Interesting," was all Snow said.

CHAPTER TWENTY-TWO

Rush

I could not believe it, and yet it felt like I should. I was not the most important person in my father's life, and while I was sure his own well-being was paramount, Fred was held up higher than I was.

"You piece of shit!" Simon was out of his seat and moving toward my father. He was quick, so fast he had my father on the ground, chair and all, before Mace, who was next to him, could stop him.

"Simon!" I shouted, but it seemed I was the only one upset about his outburst.

"Sit down, Rush." Snow waved me off. "Mace has got this, and you can't blame Eight for reacting the way he did."

Mace was holding Simon back while my father lay flat on the ground. Simon's face was bright red, and the hatred in his eyes as he glared at my father sent a shiver up my spine.

"Mr. Abernathy, if the safety of Simon and my family weren't at stake, I'd throw you to the wolves myself." Snow pushed his chair out and glared at my father. "I know shitty dads; I had one of the worst. I was alone, vulnerable, a lamb heading toward slaughter. The family I have in Simon, Christopher, others that have opened their arms to me, is everything. They found me and none of them, not one would hesitate to step in front of a bullet for me. I've known your son all of a day and I want to protect him. You've had twentysomething years with him, and you hesitate to protect him because your dick wants a too-young-for-you hole?" Snow grunted, disgust adorning his pretty features.

"I love my son." My father had made no attempt to get up, and Mace was still holding onto Simon.

"No, Mr. Abernathy, I'm not sure you do. Personally, I don't think you can comprehend the word love. Either way, my family will make sure your son walks away from this with a bright future."

"A future *he* chooses, not you," Simon snarled.

As if a switch went off in my father, he bolted up and pointed an accusatory finger at Simon. "Did you call me here to bully me into letting my son major in the arts?"

I was not sure who was more astounded by that question, me or everyone else.

"Father, why would someone do all of this just so I could major in the arts? Regardless of anything, it doesn't change that Fred is the son of a mobster, one who frowns on him being gay, and you're having sex with him."

My father's nostrils flared, and he narrowed his eyes. "So, I lose my job and possibly die at the hands of a mob boss?"

"These are choices you've made, Mr. Abernathy." Snow looked up at my father from his seated position. "You had to know that sleeping with a student was wrong…you know, since your family helped establish the rules."

One of the servers came and righted the fallen chair, and my father sat down. Mace released Simon and he went to his chair as well, but not without a disdainful glare in my father's direction.

"Fred lights something up inside me. I don't think of repercussions when I'm with him, just that being there, in that moment, is the most freeing feeling I've ever known."

Seeing my father dejected and so in touch with his feelings was hard to watch. I felt both sorry for him and angry. Sorry because I could see he was truly under a spell with Fred. Angry because I wondered if he'd ever loved my mother that much...or me.

"Mr. Abernathy, I'm not here to help you with the school board. Honestly, that's a battle you need to fight on your own. I'm merely here to keep people alive. I doubt you have a lot of experience speaking with people like Liam Brennan."

"No, I..." My father furrowed his brow, his gaze locked on to the table. He appeared lost. "Perhaps if you convince Liam to understand, he will tell the board it wasn't true?"

It was Simon who spoke, and while not red-faced anymore, his anger was evident. "First, you assume Liam was the one who told the board. You have no proof of that."

"But you could ask, couldn't you?"

Simon rolled his eyes. "These are high school games. The board is your problem. What Liam rescinds or doesn't in that regard is up to him."

My father looked as if he were seeing me for the first time. There was a subtle softness in his features, but I knew him to be a viper at times.

"I suppose if you have opinions about me and this situation, now would be as good a time as any to air them." His words were clipped, almost as if he were daring me to say one thing in the negative about him and Fred.

"I think my opinions don't matter to you. But if you want to talk about this, we should do that in private be—"

"Private!" my father shouted. "You dragged my personal life

out in the open right here in this room. Now, you want to do me the courtesy of privacy?"

"I didn't do that; you did that when you made your choices. Honestly, Father, if this were just about you sleeping with a student, it would just be the two of us. But it's not; it's about you sleeping with a mob boss's son and him wanting to kill me, and probably you. Now, I don't know about your expertise, but I certainly don't know how to negotiate with the Mafia, do you?"

I could tell my father had zero clue how to do that, but he was going to make sure to push this as far away from him as possible. "You do realize your boyfriend is the reason anyone is shining a light on this, right?"

"Are you seriously spinning this?" Simon argued. "You fucked a student, and yeah, my family did some digging into people surrounding me and him to see if it was safe to bring Rush in so he could meet my pops and know who I was. All things that your son had no knowledge of. So, maybe stop projecting!"

Mace chuckled. "Sure you're not taking psych classes?"

Simon shrugged. "Took one once."

"Mr. Abernathy, you either work with us, or you're going to be dealing with this on your own." Snow nodded to the servers, who placed some salad and soup in front of us. My appetite had disappeared, but I didn't want to be disrespectful, so I picked.

"I'm not sure what you need from me." My father only glanced at the food but showed no move to eat anything.

"I need you to do exactly what I tell you to do." Snow poured some dressing on his salad.

"Fine, and what would that be?"

"Showing some respect, for starters," Bill grumbled.

My father blushed, embarrassed or nervous I couldn't tell. I focused on my food, knowing it probably tasted amazing, but everything was ash in my mouth.

"You have to go before the board, correct?" Snow asked.

"Yes, tomorrow. It's a preliminary of sorts."

Snow nodded as he popped a cherry tomato into his mouth. "You have counsel?"

"I do."

"What I need you to do is discuss with your counsel that you need as much information as possible. What proof they have that you had relations with Fred, and see if they know who reported it."

"I was going to do that anyway." My father could only hold back his snobbery for so long, but any sign that Snow was angered by it did not show on his face.

"Stay the hell away from Fred. Even if he contacts you begging and saying all the things that rev your engine. Stay put and tell him no. I don't have the manpower to guard you, so don't give Liam a reason to shoot you."

My father's eyes widened. "And what if he shows up, or one of his goons do?"

Bill chuckled. "Goons?"

"Bill, please." Snow smirked. "I suggest dialing 9-1-1."

"Snow." Simon said his name softly. "Cops?"

"Look, I know my father is impossible, but I don't want him to die. Is there anything you can do to keep him safe?" As angry as I was, I didn't want him to die.

Snow released a breath, wiped his mouth, and regarded my father. "I will talk with my husband, and he will decide on this. In the meantime, be careful. It's the best I can offer you."

"Be careful?" My father looked around the table. "Can't we call Fred and meet with him? Maybe he can help."

"You don't call the head of the Irish mob's son without permission," Simon answered.

"If Fred was shunned for his homosexuality, I would think he'd be grateful for the help." My father was more defensive about Fred than anything to do with me, and if it were just the two of us, I would have walked out by now.

"Not a chance I'm willing to take for my family." Snow lifted a single silver brow. "Family actually means something to me."

"It means something to me too."

Simon scoffed at my father. "You have a shit way of showing it."

"I'm trying to—"

"Never mind," Snow said loudly. "I will use the correct channels to speak with Fred, and I will speak with my husband about your safety."

There was not much left to say after that; we were in a holding pattern until Snow spoke with Christopher. As we ate, quietly, my father kept glancing around the table at everyone. He was jumpy and wouldn't make eye contact with me once.

By the time we were done eating, you could cut the tension with a knife.

"Well, I must be going." He did not thank anyone or pay. He walked right out of the room without even acknowledging me.

My stomach roiled and abruptly, I ran to the nearest bathroom. What had my life become?

CHAPTER TWENTY-THREE

Simon

Rush shooed me out of the bathroom when I followed, and I was not about to argue with him. Seeing how his dad had treated him nearly had me beating him bloody. Currently, I was standing outside the bathroom, scowling. No one was trying to get in, but I would stop them if they did. Rush needed time.

"It's sort of strange." Snow came up beside me, leaning against the wall.

"What's strange?"

"You had the most loving household growing up, and it was the home of a mobster." He smiled as if it were the funniest thing. "Rush and I had law-abiding fathers…well, at least to the outside world, they were. Mine was a police chief and his was the namesake of a prestigious university. Both pieces of shit."

"Goes to show, you can't judge a person by their occupation." I shrugged, my head thunking on the hard surface.

"You didn't ask me once why I was here instead of Christopher."

I turned and looked down at Snow. He was genuinely curious as to why. "I never wondered."

"But why not? I mean, he's the head of the family, your blood."

I rolled my eyes so hard it hurt. "Snow, Pops doesn't see you as anything other than his equal, and all his associates know it. I know he has a shit-ton of stuff to do, and I don't think he loves me less than you do because you're here and he's not."

"Well." Snow smirked. "I totally love you more than he does."

Chuckling, I elbowed him lightly. "I'm grateful you came."

"There was never a doubt one of us would."

The door to the bathroom opened. Rush was pale as a ghost, and he had a pained look on his face.

"You okay, sweet boy?" Snow went right over to him and cupped his face.

It tore me apart when Rush's eyes filled, and he shook his head. He was breaking and trying so hard not to.

Snow placed one of his hands on Rush's chest. "This is shattering right now, and you have to let the pieces fall where they may. It's only after the shards have landed that someone will pick them up and put them together again. And the cracks and fissures will always show. They will tell the tale of all you've endured. But that person who made your heart whole again will be its protector, and their love will never let it shatter again."

Rush's eyes flickered to mine, and I hoped he wanted that person to be me.

"I want to believe you." Rush's voice was hoarse, whether from being sick or emotional, I didn't know.

"Time will help with that." Snow patted his cheek and left the two of us alone.

I moved closer to Rush, not knowing what to say but desperate to make him feel better. He looked at me, sadness and hurt shining through, and then he threw his arms around me and I held him while he silently cried.

Rush and I were driving to the dorms, Mace following behind in his car, when all hell broke loose. There was no other way to describe it. The radio was on low, Rush was staring out the window, stuck in his head. The light in front of me turned green, I hit the gas, and a car crashed into me on the driver's side.

"What the hell?" Rush shouted. I was trying to control my car, which was currently spinning.

I slammed on the brakes, and the sound of screeching metal and the smell of burning rubber filled the car.

"Get down!" I shouted to Rush.

"Down, why? I—"

"Just do it." I pressed my hand on his head, urging him to listen, glad when he did. A second slam hit from behind, urging my car forward and through a store window. I could hear gunfire, screaming, and the sounds of utter destruction around me.

I pulled the lever on the left-hand side, under the light controls, for the emergency brake, desperate to stop my car before it went through the brick wall in front of me. Rush was yelling incoherently. Looking out the rear window, I saw a large black SUV barreling toward me. I jerked the wheel to the left, so the front of the SUV was facing my side. I could see the passenger lift his hand and point a gun at me. I ducked and grabbed the Colt 1911 I had under my seat.

"Stay low, Rush, please." I saw the terror in his eyes, that fight-or-flight ever present in people when situations like this arise. I needed him to listen to me because if he darted out of my car, I didn't know if I would be able to stop a bullet from claiming him.

He didn't answer, just ducked his head, arms and hands wrapping around his face and ears when another round of bullets rained over the windshield of my car. The second they stopped, I lifted my head, pointed my gun at the driver, and shot him point-blank between the eyes.

The passenger got out of the SUV, and I could see him running toward me. I raised my Colt again, but a shot rang out and he fell forward. Mace stood less than a foot behind him, blood dripping down his face.

There were sirens in the distance, Rush was huddled on the floor of my car, and there was a lot to figure out.

"Simon." Mace raced up to my car. "You guys okay?"

One look over at Rush and we both knew, while physically he was okay, he was in shock. "You gotta get out of here, Mace. Take this." I handed him my Colt.

"How are you going to explain this?" Mace's gaze roamed over all the mess. The store must not have been open, or everyone had scattered; all I saw were the two dead guys and a shit-ton of bricks and glass.

"Let me figure it out. Get your car out of here, I know you won't go far, but get far enough that they can't see you. Go, hurry."

I knew he despised the idea, but Mace would get arrested. He was out of Pops's jurisdiction and reach here. But me, I was supposedly a law-abiding citizen and Rush...well, his family were saints in the eyes of this town.

When Mace was out of sight and driving his car, which looked a lot better than mine, I reached to tap Rush on the hand. He jumped and screamed.

"Hey, it's okay. It's safe." I hoped I wasn't lying.

"Safe!" he shouted without moving from the floor. "There were bullets."

"Yeah."

"You…" He glanced past me, I wasn't sure what he was seeing. Slowly he rose, sitting on the passenger seat even though it was covered in glass. "You killed a guy."

"I did, but, Rush, you can't tell the police that."

He cocked his head, clearly confused, but I had no time to say more. Cops, fire department, and ambulances showed up, and I crossed everything I had in the hopes that he would let me handle it.

With my head against the headrest and my eyes closed, I listened to the police and EMTs as they made their way through the rubble. Rush's breathing was calming down, and he no longer appeared to be about to freak out. He was, however, facing away from the dead bodies, and I was sure he was wishing he were Dorothy wishing she were back in Kansas.

CHAPTER TWENTY-FOUR

Rush

When I was a little kid, my mother took me to this ice cream shop with stools that spun. I loved lying on my belly and spinning over and over until I was dizzy and staring at the ceiling, seeing all the shapes twirl. The problem was, I would get sick and had to force down the ice cream or else she would never let me go there again.

The last hour gave me all the same feelings but without the ice cream. I was dizzy, nauseous, my adrenaline was spiking, and while exciting, it was terrifying.

The EMTs walked me over to the ambulance since I was okay to do so. They asked me questions like what was my name, what day is it, who is the President? I answered as if on autopilot.

Over one of their shoulders, I saw Simon getting a bandage on his arm while talking to a police officer. Did he get shot? What was he saying to the cops? What the hell should I tell them?

"Sir, are you feeling agitated?" one of the EMTs asked.

"I was just in a war zone; of course I'm agitated."

"Blood pressure is elevating…" She was talking again, but I

tuned her out to watch Simon and the police officer. I really wished I could hear what he was telling him because I knew I had to make my story match up.

What the fuck was wrong with me? Simon had killed a man. I knew he had, and that Mace guy had too, but looking at Simon over there talking to the police officer, he was calm. Was that not the first person he had ever killed? It wasn't something you could just ask someone, and maybe he wouldn't tell me, plausible deniability and all that.

"Mr. Abernathy, I'm Sergeant Quinn. I wanted to ask you a few questions."

Shit. "Oh, okay."

He nodded. "Do you know who the men who died are?"

That was easy. "No, I've never seen them before."

"All right, and can you give me a brief explanation of what happened here?"

Swallowing, I looked over and saw Simon give me a small smile. A silly thing in the middle of all this mess but it oddly warmed me. A strange strength came over me. I knew those men had hit us and shot at us, and I knew Simon had kept me alive.

"Simon and I were driving back from lunch and we were at the intersection a little ways from the restaurant, I think it's Clay Avenue? Not sure. Anyway, Simon hit the gas and this car, well, SUV, I guess, hit us."

"You guess?"

"It happened so fast. We were hit, we spun. Simon was worried about me and told me to duck, so I did."

"Like a head to your knees sort of thing?" The officer was writing everything on a little pad, and I hoped I was coming off believable.

"Yeah, I heard so much metal and glass. It was loud, but I stayed where I was instructed."

"Did you see anything after the SUV hit you?"

"No, Sergeant. Like I said, I had my head down. Only when the car stopped and I heard the sirens did I sit up."

"There are bullet holes in the Mercedes and in the SUV. Did you hear gunfire?"

I closed my eyes, mainly because I did not want to have to look at him when I lied.

"No, I mean maybe, I can't be sure. I'm sorry."

He wrote something else down, thanked me, and went over to where Simon was talking to who I assumed was his partner.

"You seem to be okay, just a little shaken up. Take it easy for the rest of the day."

I nodded and saw two men dressed in suits approach Simon. I pegged them for detectives.

"Can I go now? I'd like to see if my boyfriend is okay."

"Just take it easy."

I slid off the bed of the ambulance and walked over to Simon. As I got closer, I could hear them all talking.

"How did these two men end up dying from gunshot wounds?" one of the detectives asked.

"How am I supposed to know? They hit my car and tried to kill me. We were spinning, and I remember pulling the emergency brake so we wouldn't slam into that brick wall." He gestured behind himself, where his car was maybe three inches from said wall.

"But these men are dead, there is one hole in the driver's head, and one in the passenger's. How does that happen in a car accident?"

"Excuse me," I said, making five sets of eyes turn and stare at me. "How do you know these men died from being shot?"

Silence. Likely because they thought I was a moron.

"Rushmore Abernathy?" one of the detectives asked.

"The Third, yes."

"Right. So, the holes in their heads tell that story." He turned to Simon, but I was not done.

"Did they do both autopsies here on the pavement?"

Simon's brows reached his hairline, and the cops and detectives looked irritated.

"Of course not!"

"Then you don't really know what killed them, how they died, or anything, actually."

"I've been doing this for a real long time." The detective had moved closer to me.

"Then you understand how this works. See, what I know is, Simon and I were driving to the dorms after a wonderful lunch when this monster car hit us. The way I see it is, we were the victims, and here you are berating us for what, not being shot in the head?"

"That's not my intention, but the way this all looks—"

I sidled next to Simon and took his hand in mine. "We were in a horrific accident, Simon has injuries, and we need to rest. Unless you're planning on arresting us for driving home, I suggest you let us return to our dorms and sleep. We both need to go see a doctor in the morning per the EMT's instructions, and it seems we need a lawyer too." I narrowed my eyes at the detective, enjoying the surge of power that came over me.

"Let 'em go, Gerry," the older detective said.

"How are you getting there? I can drive you," Sergeant Quinn offered.

"I appreciate that, but driving up to campus in a cop car isn't exactly easy to explain. We just want to sleep. I called for an Uber. Thanks."

Simon and I did not talk as we walked over toward the curb. I hadn't called an Uber service, but as soon as we were away from the police, Simon texted Mace and two minutes later, he was driving up to get us. His car, while sustaining some damage, wasn't any worse looking than a vehicle that had one too many dings.

Only after we drove away from the scene did I release the breath I hadn't realized I'd been holding.

"Are you both okay?" Mace was glaring out the windshield, and I could see from my seat in the back, he was white-knuckling the wheel.

"I'm fine." I looked over at Simon. "How are you?"

"Got a piece of glass in my arm, but I'll live."

"This is bad, Simon."

For some reason when a man like Mace said that, it instilled a kind of fear in me I had never felt.

"I know." Simon took my hand in his and squeezed lightly. "You were great over there, and I know you're probably regretting ever coming over to me at the bar that night."

His hands were crusted with dried blood, his own I was sure, and as I glided my thumb over his, I realized that as awful as today was, how terrible my father was being, I did not regret meeting Simon.

"It's hard to believe it's only been a little over two weeks since we met. It feels like forever."

Simon hummed. "Yeah, I remember when Snow and my pops met, and one night I heard Snow talking to Frank—he works for Pops too. And Snow said the same thing."

"Care to elaborate?" I wanted to listen to anything other than the voices in my head telling me to freak out.

"My pops fell fast and hard for Snow, but there were a lot of trust issues on Snow's side of things. He couldn't believe how easy it was to love Pops. I think he'd never felt anything like it and was having a hard time reconciling it."

"Falling hard and fast?" I quirked a brow.

Simon lifted my hand to his mouth and pressed a soft kiss to my knuckles. "I'm crazy about you, Rushmore Abernathy the Third."

CHAPTER TWENTY-FIVE

Rush

He was crazy about me. I thought about that the entire way to the university. He didn't press me to respond, which I was grateful for, and even when I became quiet after his confession, he let me be. Crazy about me. He'd killed a man, and I was actually not having a hard time with that. Maybe there was something wrong with me.

"You two stay in your room tonight." Mace pulled his car into the spot normally reserved for Simon's car. "I was going to bring you to the hotel, but Bill said not to. It's not any safer until we have more manpower."

Mace and Simon both got out of the car, and I rounded the side in time to hear Simon ask, "More manpower?"

Mace huffed and started walking toward my dorms. "Mace." Simon was limping slightly, which had me worried.

"Simon, why are you limping?"

That made Mace stop and turn. "You're more hurt than you led the EMT to believe, aren't you?"

Simon waved Mace away. "Answer me."

"I want to see your leg when we get in the room." He said no more and kept walking. It was stupid to talk so openly anyway, so we followed at a pace that was easier on Simon.

By the time we got to my dorm, Simon was sweating, and not from exertion but definitely from pain, judging by his pinched expression. Mace opened the door and Simon went right over to the bed and collapsed.

"Let me see." Mace kneeled by his side, helping Simon remove his pants. "Shit, Simon."

I moved closer to see. His entire left leg was bruising, and his ankle was swelling like a balloon. He wasn't bleeding, and it had gone unnoticed because there were no tears in his pants.

"It didn't seem so bad until the adrenaline began to fade. When I pulled the emergency brake, I pushed my knee out of the way, and the door crushed my leg. That has to be how it happened."

"I'm going to go get some ice. Rush, help Simon get comfortable. Elevate the leg and if you have any pain medicine, that would be great."

I nodded to Mace. "There's a little convenience store next to the cafeteria, they sell ice there, and they're still open."

"Got it. Lock the door behind me."

As soon as Mace left, I locked the door and went about getting Simon comfortable. I had his leg elevated and pillows behind him so he could drink the water I gave him and take the pain meds.

Mace returned with ice and went about making some ice packs using ziplock bags and socks.

"That's fucking cold," Simon hissed.

"Don't be a baby. The swelling needs to subside."

"Mace," Simon said once he was iced. "Tell me."

I had no idea what they were talking about, but I sat on the little couch and listened.

"How do you think the conversation I had with Snow about you almost dying went?"

"I didn't almost die, Mace."

"Doesn't matter what you or I think. Those two guys that hit your car, we ran the plates. Owner is Liam Brennan. They were patsies but it's a message sent, and Christopher has received it."

"Fuck." Simon's head fell against the pillow, and I didn't understand the problem.

"Can you two dumb it down for the non-mafioso in the room?"

"Liam Brennan almost killed Simon, and you. It was a two-birds-one-stone kind of thing. See, Liam is pissed at your old man. And Christopher is a big fish. One that if Brennan made a mark on, word would get around. Make him a bigger fish than Christopher."

"But I'm alive, and so is Simon."

"Something I'm sure Liam won't be thrilled with, but it got Christopher's attention and now…"

I looked between the two men. "And now, what?"

"Now my pops is coming to town."

Christopher Manos is coming here? Maybe that would be a good thing.

"That's great! He can make it all stop. Talk to Liam, maybe fix all this crap."

"You don't get it," Simon said. "He's not coming here to fix it, he's coming here to end it. There's absolutely nothing Liam Brennan could say to Pops that would make him not kill the Irish shit."

"But that…won't that—"

"Start a war? Yeah." Simon closed his eyes and pinched the bridge of his nose.

"You had to know it was always going to come to that." Mace sat on the edge of the bed. "A man like Liam Brennan doesn't just say 'Pardon me, excuse me, my apologies,' and scurry off. No, he's a bull. He'd tell Christopher one thing and do another. We always knew this."

"Then why make anyone believe it could work out? Why did Snow say he'd keep me safe?"

Mace and Simon both looked at me, and I knew. I just fucking knew. Yes, they were going to keep me safe, but they'd always known there was going to be a war.

"Oh," I whispered.

"Rush, I'm so sorry."

I saw Simon try to get out of bed to come over to me, but Mace pushed him back down. "Stay. Listen, Rush, I get it. You're thinking all this shit in that brain about what this means. When it ends, and it will end, what will you do? That's going to be up to you. Christopher won't stop you from living your life. You're not part of the problem."

I could see the pain in Simon's eyes. "But Simon won't stay here." I couldn't explain how I knew that. How Christopher Manos being here and starting something with Liam Brennan would mean the end of his time here.

"I don't think he'll be able to, no."

"Rush, wherever I go, you can come with me if you want."

There was a moment of silence before Mace stood. "I'm going to be outside your room."

I wanted to tell Mace to stay, because where the hell would he sit out there? But in that moment, I couldn't speak; it felt like a vise was squeezing my heart to the point of pain. What Simon was saying was heavy, and I hadn't realized how much I wanted that.

"Maybe we don't decide anything tonight." Simon opened his arms. "We need to sleep and since I'm taking up most of the bed, and that couch is far too small for you, you'll have to lie on me." His lip curved, and I decided to go along with it since the reality of what tomorrow would bring was too dire.

"Okay." I stripped to my boxers and slid in next to Simon, mostly on his right side so as to not hurt his leg.

We didn't speak. He ran his fingers through my hair while I listened to the thrumming of his heartbeat. I wasn't sure I would be able to fall asleep, seeing as it wasn't that late but soon enough, my lids became heavy and sleep claimed me.

———

There are not a lot of things more jarring than feeling someone stare at you while you sleep. Simon must have woken and refused to move. So I lifted my head to see him, but his eyes were closed.

"He's always been a heavy sleeper, even as a baby." The deep-timbered voice made me jump. Over on my couch, there was a shadow of a man. It was too early, and the sun hadn't risen yet, so the room was still bathed in darkness.

"Who's there?"

The shadowed man's laugh was deep, and whiskey rough. "If I was here to harm you, you'd be dead already." He leaned forward enough for the street lamp outside to catch his face.

Christopher Manos was easily an older version of Simon. A small smile played on his lips, he had scruff that resembled more of a five o'clock shadow than a beard, and his black hair was combed back. He was in a dark suit, and every part of his being screamed power.

"Holy shit!" I vocalized my shock a little louder than I intended, making Simon jolt.

"What, holy shit what?" He squinted at me, then reached for his glasses on the nightstand. Once they were on, he saw Christopher.

"Jesus, Pops. How long you been here?"

"About an hour. Nice to see you too."

As carefully as I could, I slid to the side of the bed, keeping myself covered. Simon tried to get up, but Christopher came to him and wrapped Simon in an engulfing hug.

"I don't like when you make me worry about you."

"Sorry, Pops, I didn't mean to."

Christopher huffed and returned to the couch. He looked at me again and smiled. "What is it with the Manos men and falling for guys who almost get us killed?"

"I blame you." Simon was laughing.

"You little shit."

I realized the ice packs on Simon's ankle were melted, so I removed them. As I tossed them into the trash, I could feel Christopher's gaze on me.

"A lot of people have to answer for things," he said.

"Isn't there a way to do this peacefully?" Simon sat up more and snagged a T-shirt that was near him. It was one of mine, and fortunately it was clean.

"I don't want any of this, Simon. But I have to end this on my terms, or every boss will think there is an end to my reach. I can't have that."

"I don't get something. If the SUV was registered to Liam Brennan, why not let the police handle it? They'll see Brennan is responsible and take it from there."

Christopher shook his head. "Those cops, the ones you all talked to? Those are Liam's cops. This will magically disappear as some deadly drinking and driving incident. Nothing more."

It was so scary to see how powerful these men were.

"Since Simon's rude"—Christopher held his hand out to me—"I'm Christopher Manos, Nice to meet you."

"Oh!" I quickly shook his hand. "I'm Rush."

"Now, I'm going to step out and talk to Mace. You two get dressed, because we're leaving."

I jumped out of bed, just in my boxers. "Leaving? Where are we going?"

Christopher moved toward the door. "Someplace a hell of a lot safer than here."

CHAPTER TWENTY-SIX

Simon

The safe place my pops was referring to was a house he'd decided to rent on the fly. He'd used an alias and paid for three months in advance even though he would only need a few days. The landlord lived in another state and wouldn't need to deal with collecting rent or bothering with us.

"Who just comes to town and rents a house?" Rush whispered in my ear as we sat in the living room while Christopher finished a phone call.

"My family."

"Okay." Christopher sat down on the large wingback chair next to the fireplace. "Snow has kept me informed of everything going on, so I'm caught up. Here's what's going to happen next. I will schedule a meeting with Liam and make him think I'm willing to do things his way. In the meantime, Simon and Rush, you're going to get both Fred and Rush's father here."

"Whoa," Rush said. "How are we going to do that? Fred won't listen to anyone, and they aren't allowed to be near each other. Snow even told my father that."

"And then Liam tried to get you both killed. That's a game changer."

"Getting Rush's father here won't be hard, I'm sure. But how do we get Fred to come?"

"Wait, I got it, actually," Rush said in answer to my question. "I can't believe I didn't think of it, but we can send an email to Fred and say it's my father, and he wants to meet but at a place they won't be seen."

"What if they've been talking and it doesn't work?"

Rush rolled his eyes and I chuckled. "We hope for the best. But if I know my father at all, I suspect he's been ignoring Fred."

"Okay, good plan." Christopher sat back. "Let me call Liam now."

"Now?" Rush looked at me. "What…"

"Good morning, Liam, it's Christopher Manos. I believe you are aware of who I am. If not, perhaps you remember my nephew. He was the man you had your men drive off the road and try and kill. Ring any bells?"

Rush stared at Christopher both in awe and like he was insane. Honestly, you had to be a little insane to be a mob boss.

"Right, I don't give a shit about who is fucking who and where. What I do give a shit about is that you dared to order a hit on my nephew, and you think that won't go unpaid."

Rush leaned closer to me and spoke softly. "This is the business you want to work in? Really?"

I smiled because he asked as if I'd told him I wanted to be a dancer. It was not how he saw me, but he was trying to respect my choices.

"It's in my blood, Rush. But I won't ask you to be part of it. I'd never force that."

"Tomorrow at one will work. We need to have a sit-down and figure out how to end this." Christopher's voice was loud, and Rush slunk away a little. "Until then." He disconnected the call.

"Need a computer?" I asked Rush, who nodded. "Okay, hang on." I was sure someone had brought a laptop with them. I went toward the rear of the house, glad my ankle was on the mend and the swelling had dissipated and not returned. It was sore but I felt a lot better than I did the day before. I found Snow and Bill talking in one of the rooms.

"Hey, Eight."

"Hi, can I borrow your laptop?"

He nodded and took it out of the case. "If you watch weird porn, please delete the browser history; I don't need the nightmares of never being able to forget the things that turn you on."

I snatched it out of his hand and left, giving him the finger on my way out.

"I'd spank you for that if I was sure you wouldn't enjoy it!" he shouted just as I rounded the corner to the living room, where Christopher and Rush were staring at me.

"Don't look at me like that, Pops. You married that man."

"And he's the luckiest man in the world for that," Snow yelled.

"Damn right." Christopher's cheesy grin was all a person needed to see when talking to or about his husband. They were sickeningly in love.

"Here you go, Rush. If you fear you may be sick due to the disgusting display of affection Snow and Pops are showing each other, we can find a different room."

Surprisingly, Rush laughed. "No, it's nice, actually. My parents never really showed their love publicly."

"Okay, but if you change your mind let me know."

I sat beside him while he went into his father's email account and sent a message off to Fred. "I'm surprised your father gave you the password to his email."

Rush huffed. "It's been the same password ever since I can remember, and it's the same password he uses for everything. It shouldn't surprise him that the board found out about him and Fred."

It was the first time I had heard Rush crack a joke about his father and Fred, so I smiled at him.

"Now you have to call your father." Christopher handed him Rush's phone that had been on the table.

"Okay, but someone has to watch the email. As soon as Fred responds, erase it and toss it into the trash so my father doesn't see it."

"I'll watch it while you call your dad." I took the laptop and settled it in my lap.

Rush took a deep breath and made the call. "Hello, it's Rush...Right, you saw that on the caller ID. Anyway, I need to see you tomorrow but, look, I need you to come to a place I'm staying...No, I'm not at the dorm right now...Because there was an issue yesterday that nearly got me and Simon killed."

Christopher did not look happy that Rush had mentioned anything, but he also hadn't gotten the opportunity to meet Rush's dad. I had a feeling he would need a good reason to come to his son.

"How about one?...Yeah, I can send you the address in a text...Okay. See you tomorrow." Once he disconnected the call, he shot a text off and put his phone down.

"You did good," I said.

He shrugged, and I knew it had to do with his father just never wanting to budge on anything Rush asked for. Whether it be his career or simply getting together.

It was twenty minutes before Fred answered the email, and when he did he responded that he'd be here at one tomorrow. So, while Christopher was off meeting with Liam, we would have Fred and Rush's dad to deal with.

It was going to be a long day.

That night, after a long-ass meeting about what the following day would entail, Rush and I went up to bed. Snow had told Rush there was a room for him and one for me and to do with that information as he would.

I knew Snow was trying to give Rush a choice, and I respected that. My leg was starting to ache, so I took some pain meds and went into my room. Rush was on my bed. He had a T-shirt on and boxers…and a smile.

"I hope it's okay if I stay with you."

There was no force in this world that would have me say no to this man.

"I'm glad you're here."

I made quick work of divesting myself of my clothes down to my boxers and slipped into bed.

"How did this house become ready for people in such a short time?" Rush asked as he turned my way, resting his head on his hand.

"Never underestimate Snow. When my pops said he was on his way, I'm sure Snow was way ahead of him."

I mirrored Rush's position and smiled. His brows flickered and he reached out, lightly tracing his finger over my skin.

"Infinity," he whispered. He was referring to my tattoo that was not infinity.

"Actually, it's the number eight. I got it when I turned eighteen."

Rush chuckled. "It's funny. That's the nickname he gave you, and the number eight, you can trace it over and over forever…like infinity."

"A perfect coincidence."

"Simon, I—"

I pressed a kiss to his lips, silencing him for just a moment because I knew he might say something that would break my heart. I loved how his eyes were closed when I pulled back and I got to see them open.

Rush released a breath, a small smile appearing on his face. "Why'd you do that?"

"I didn't know what you were going to say, and if it was gonna be something that pushed us apart, I wanted one more moment with you."

"Oh, Simon."

Rush took my face in his hands and kissed me until I was lying flat. He was careful not to hurt my leg, but when he straddled me, I didn't care if it was excruciating. I'd take the pain if it meant he was touching me.

"I don't want to hurt you," he mumbled into my mouth.

"You're not."

"Simon." He pecked my lips and sat up. "I wasn't going to say good-bye to you just now. I was going to say I didn't know how tomorrow was going to go. I've never been through anything like this before. But I wanted you to know regardless of anything, I'm so glad you spilled your drink on that lady's shoes, and I don't regret meeting you."

I didn't know of anything I could say that was better than that, so I pulled him close and showed him how much he meant to me.

I spent hours licking, kissing, and sucking him. He had one fist in his mouth, trying not to scream, and the other gripped the sheets. I swallowed him to the root as I finger-fucked him, loving the keening sounds he made. Like he was on the border of pleasure and pain.

When he arched off the mattress and came down my throat, I swallowed everything he gave me, loving his taste and his vulnerability.

CHAPTER TWENTY-SEVEN

Rush

By the time Simon and I made it to the kitchen in the morning, Snow was putting breakfast on the table. I noticed some new faces and I didn't want to be rude, so I greeted everyone and introduced myself before taking my seat.

"Oh, that's right, these guys weren't here yesterday. Well, they were, but they were doing security things." Snow smiled as he put a plate of pancakes on the table.

"You know Bill and Mace." Bill acknowledged me by lifting up a forkful of eggs.

"This guy here is Frank; he's always with Chris and came in with him but was scoping some places out, so you didn't see him. This guy is Donny. Also came in with Chris."

"Nice to meetcha." Frank winked. He appeared to be older than Christopher and more bulk to Christopher's muscles, but he was also scary-looking until he smiled.

"Hey." Donny jerked his head and popped a piece of bacon into his mouth.

"I have pancakes, eggs, bacon, sausage, toast, fruit salad—"

"We got it, Snow, sit and eat." Simon gave him a look of such adoration I had to avert my gaze.

"I just want everyone nice and full before they head out." Snow sat in his chair and Christopher walked in, dressed impeccably in a black Hugo Boss suit. My father would approve.

"Good morning, everyone." He bent and gave Snow a kiss.

"Morning," everyone grumbled as if the most terrifying man in the world hadn't just waltzed in here.

"How'd you sleep?"

I looked up and realized he was talking to me.

"Oh, um fine, why?"

He chuckled as he took his seat beside Snow. "You're so jumpy. I was just wondering since the fucking train kept me up all night." I hadn't heard a train but then again, Simon and I had only slept maybe two hours. If he wasn't fucking me, I was fucking him.

"I didn't hear a train," Mace said with a mouth full of pancake.

"Because you fucking snore louder than one." Bill elbowed Mace, which made Mace elbow him and...wow, they were like children. Suddenly, I was laughing so hard my belly hurt.

I wasn't sure how long I laughed, but it felt like forever and I just couldn't stop. When I wiped away my tears and looked around the table, they were all staring at me.

"What?"

"Are you okay?" Simon squeezed my hand.

"Me? I'm fine...fine, really. What would be wrong? I mean, it's not like it's the last day my father will ever talk to me or that maybe someone gets killed or anything like that, no. It's great. I see all of you acting like it's a regular boring day, no fear, nothing, why should I panic if you're not, right?"

"Dude, what you're doing…that's panicking." Mace pointed at Rush in a "Look at yourself" gesture.

"Maybe shut up, Mace." Bill threw a strawberry at his forehead, and it bounced off and landed in my orange juice.

"Look." Snow stood up. "We all panic, and we all do it our ways. You, Rush, babble and verbally get it out. Some people run away in the middle of the night, tell their mortal enemy and later best friend a plan that you concocted in the hopes of keeping everyone safe and end up in the trunk of a car. I'm just saying, we cope how we do, so maybe everyone can cut Rush some slack." And he plopped back down in his chair and resumed eating.

"That was oddly specific." I tilted my head, eying the man.

Simon pointed to Bill. "Mortal enemy turned best friend." He gestured to Snow. "Runaway who ended up in the trunk."

"Pointing fingers is rude," Snow snapped, then pointed directly at Simon. "You used to dip your chocolate chip cookies in apple juice like a demon."

"What the hell?" Simon dropped the bacon he was about to eat. "Are we playing this game, Snow?"

"Children." Frank laughed.

"He started it." Simon shot an accusatory finger at Snow.

"How? How did I start it? I never named names. You went all informant on us by telling Rush the whos and the whats."

"The whos and the whats?" Christopher shook his head.

"Don't betray me, Christopher!" Snow slammed a hand on the table, and everyone erupted into laughter.

———

I watched from the bay window as Christopher, Frank, and Donny got into a car and drove off to meet Liam Brennan. The clock on the mantel read twelve thirty, so we had half an hour until Fred and my father would arrive.

Bill was walking the property outside, and Mace was walking it inside. Snow was in the bedroom "getting pretty," and Simon was keeping an eye on his phone. Everything was how it should be, and if it went according to plan everything would be fine.

I was far too nervous to sit, so I spent the better part of the time pacing. If I annoyed anyone, they never said.

Mace came into the room to tell us my father had arrived. I was glad he'd come first. After the message had been sent and the call made, I was kicking myself for having them both arrive at the same time. But it worked out, and I hoped this was a sign that the whole day would go well for everyone.

Simon sent off a text to Christopher, and Mace went to Snow's room to let him know my father was here. I sat in the wingback chair that Christopher was in yesterday, and I waited.

Bill would be staying outside unless he was needed so he could keep an eye on things there. Mace would stay inside and visible.

The doorbell chimed, and Simon got up to answer it. He wasn't limping like he was last night, and he said the swelling was gone, but I still wished he could sit and relax.

"Rushmore?" I heard my father's voice before I saw him.

"Thanks for coming, Father."

He froze in the middle of the room, it appeared as if he were having some sort of internal struggle over what to do. After seeing how open Simon's family was, and how caring, it made it even more obvious how much affection I lacked from my own father. If Snow entered a room he'd go hug Simon, yet my father stood there unmoving, not coming near me.

"Of course I came. You said you were nearly killed." I noticed how he looked me up and down. "You seem fine."

"We're okay. It was dangerous all the same, and the intention was to kill us." Simon went back to his spot on the couch. "Why don't you have a seat, Mr. Abernathy."

"Rushmore, what's all this about?"

Then the doorbell chimed again, and Mace walked through the room. "Got it."

"I'm terribly confused about—" My father's words were cut off when Fred entered the room.

He wore confusion well. I was sure that when Mace opened the door Fred thought he was at the wrong location…until he saw my father. Now there was slight panic, possibly terror on his face.

"Fred, I presume?" Simon smiled and the resemblance to Christopher was uncanny. If Simon took off his glasses, he'd be a younger carbon copy.

"You presume correctly…I'm a little turned around, I'm afraid." Fred was choosing his words carefully. My father's jaw had dropped, and I was sure things were going to get messy.

"I don't think so, Fred. I'm Simon, and you've been invited. Have a seat." Simon gestured to the open spot on the couch beside him. "Mr. Abernathy, there's another chair in the corner. Perhaps you should have a seat too, and we can explain what's going on here."

Fred reluctantly sat, and my father retrieved the chair and sat too.

"Can someone explain what's going on here? I received a message from your dad, Rush, that he needed to speak with me and was given this address. And while he is in fact here, so are you."

Fred was being somewhat kind to me, but I'd learned that when he felt out of control or at a disadvantage he acted differently. Also, he probably didn't want to look like a shit in front of my father.

"Fred, I want you to listen very carefully to me, can you do that?" Simon asked.

"If it means you tell me what's going on, then yes."

"Okay. My name is Simon Manos. Now, I don't know how

much you follow the news, or your own father's affairs but the Manos name means a lot where I come from."

Fred's eyes widened, and I knew he understood exactly who Simon was and what the Manos name meant.

"I'm aware of who you are."

"And I'm well aware of who you are, Fred Brennan, son to Liam Brennan, the boss of the Irish Mafia here in these parts."

Fred's face turned red, but it wasn't anger—it was embarrassment. "I'm not part of my dad's life."

"Well, your father tried to kill me and Simon, and a big part of that was because of you."

"I...what? Why? I don't understand what either of you has to do with me."

The entire time, my father simply sat there watching the conversation. Fred looked over at him here and there, but when he kept his mouth shut he would turn away.

"I'll give you the quick version, and if you want to know more when I'm done, I'll expand on the story." Simon took a breath and was every bit the powerful man his uncle was. "You're fucking Rush's dad. I know it, we all know it. Your father found out. He's pissed. My family was poking around at the people in Rush's life to see if he was worthy of being pulled into my circle. In doing so, we caught your father's attention. He hated that and decided he wanted this all to go away. So, he had some of his men try to run Rush and me off the road, but it went poorly for them—we lived, they died."

I wasn't sure Fred was breathing; he was as still as a statue. I thought we'd have to kick him or something but, as if knowing my intentions, he snapped out of it. "You're going to kill me?"

Simon huffed. "Christopher Manos is having a sit-down with your father. We're going to see how that goes, and then we will figure out what to do with you."

"You think kidnapping me will make my father give you what you want?" He laughed. "My being here doesn't keep you safe. If anything it puts a bigger bull's-eye on you."

"We'll see." Simon got comfortable.

CHAPTER TWENTY-EIGHT

Simon

It was awkward as fuck. Fred kept watching Rush's dad, and Rush was desperately trying to come off like he didn't want to strangle Fred right there on the carpet.

I was about to offer drinks to everyone when my phone rang. It was Frank.

"Hey."

"Hi, kid. Listen, Christopher wanted me to call you. He's still talkin' to Liam, but, Simon, he has some serious shit on the Abernathy family, and I dunno if he's more pissed that his son is gay or that he's fuckin' an Abernathy."

"I don't understand. Aren't they a household name?"

Rush was looking at me, probably trying to figure out what I was talking about.

"That's what I thought—fuck, we all thought it. But a huge red flag should have hit us in the balls when we found out Papa Rush was getting his dick wet by a barely legal student."

"Can you elaborate?"

I met Mace's gaze as he stood in the archway. I knew he'd sensed things could go sideways.

"Liam has connections in this town like Christopher has in Haven Hart, you know?"

"Yeah."

"What do you know about Rush's mother's death?"

And this is where I was going to have to walk out of the room. "Hang on, Frank." I stood. "I gotta take this call. Mace, maybe drinks?"

Mace rolled his eyes, hating that I'd made him a barmaid. I left the room and went down the hall.

"Okay, Frank. I can talk. I know from what Rush told me that she killed herself and his dad found her."

Frank chuckled darkly. "Not so much." I listened in absolute horror as Frank filled me in on everything Liam had against the Abernathys. Rush's dad played innocent and aloof really fucking well, but by the time Frank finished talking, I realized Rush's father was far from those things. A few feet away sat a man more cunning than any of us realized.

"Simon, your uncle wants you to be careful. Abernathy is slick; I wouldn't be surprised if he's carrying. Fucker had us thinking he didn't even know how to use one of those things."

"I gotta go, Frank. You all be safe, get here as soon as you can."

I disconnected, calmed my pulse—because my heart was damn near beating out of my chest—and walked out of the room and returned to the living room.

Snow was sitting in the spot I vacated, telling everyone a story about his dogs, and Fred was laughing. Rush had a small smile on his face, but Mr. Abernathy was glaring…at me.

"Oh, Eight, there you are. We're having lemonade. Want one?"

"No, thanks, Snow." I walked around the room and stopped beside Mace.

"Okay, so where was I?" Snow went on with his story, and I knew it was to keep them distracted while I talked to Mace.

"What's up?" he asked while he kept his eyes on the room.

"You need to get Bill on the alert. Pops is finishing up and then he'll get over here."

"Okay, but why does Bill need to be ready, and for what?"

Snow kept sneaking glances at us, and I knew he could read our body language enough to know I didn't want them hearing. So he became more boisterous.

"Seems Rush's father isn't the wilted little flower we all thought him to be." I told Mace just enough to understand why Liam Brennan did what he did and how Rushmore Abernathy the Second might be more lethal than the Irish mob boss.

"I'm not staying here," Rush's father shouted over Snow's story. "It seems the grievance is between Fred and his father, not me. Why I'm here makes no sense."

"Sit down, Father!" Rush got up and moved toward his dad.

"No. Did I sleep with Fred? Yes, so what? He's an adult. And his father reported me to the board. Whatever his reasons, I will defend them and earn innocence."

"And what do you do for the university, Mr. Abernathy?" I stepped closer to the man, wanting his attention on me and not his son.

"Do?"

"You see, I couldn't figure out what your title was. Even when I came up to your office that day, no nameplate, nothing. It was so bizarre."

"I'm an Abernathy. One of us is always employed by the university. It builds morale and school spirit to see the Abernathy bloodlines thriving."

Rush cocked his head toward his father. "You know, that's a

good question. I don't know what you do exactly. I mean, there have been Abernathys employed at the university, but they were heads of departments, professors, for over a decade Aunt Eileen was the dean. But I don't know your title."

"Rushmore, don't listen to this man. He's obviously scheming something. Come with me, get away from this madness. Why would you get wrapped up with a Mafia family?"

"I could ask the same thing about you." I looked over at Snow, who wasn't moving. He was taking in the room, Fred, everything.

"Why, because of Fred?" he scoffed. "Please."

"Why do you say my name like that?" Fred stood, and great, now there were too many bodies in motion.

"Like what?"

"Like I disgust you? I wasn't the one who seduced you. You came on to me."

Rush's father rolled his eyes. "We had fun. Clearly, no more can come of it. As it is, being with you could cost me my job."

"What's going on, Father?" Rush sounded desperate, as if he knew his father was hiding something, something sinister, but was hoping he was wrong.

"Why is everyone ganging up on me?" He took a few steps away from us and stood by the bay window.

"You have a lot to answer for, Mr. Abernathy." I reached behind my back, where my gun rested in my waistband. I wanted to be ready.

"The hell I do."

Carefully I inched closer to Rush, to block him from his father's line of sight. "You had us all going, you know. I mean, when I met you, you were so pretentious. But you didn't know who I was, did you?"

"What are you blathering about?" he snapped.

"When you did find out I was a Manos and were stuck in a

private room with us, you put on a good show of being afraid and unknowing of the dark side of the moon. Didn't you?"

"Simon, what's going on?"

I wanted so much to take Rush into a room and explain it all to him, but the time for that wouldn't come. He was going to find out how evil his father was, how terrible the name he was attached to really was, right here in this living room.

"Rush, this is one of those you-have-to-trust-me moments."

"Rushmore, come over here. Get away from him. He's dangerous and trying to push you toward his insane way of thinking."

When he approached, I held my hand up, stopping him. "You're going to stay right there, Mr. Abernathy."

"I've had just about enough of this!"

I gripped his arm and pushed him. When he fell, he slammed into the wall, making a hell of a dent.

"Simon!" Rush tried to go to him, but I wrapped my arms around him.

"Rush, no, please."

"This isn't what we discussed."

"Because I didn't know. None of us did."

"Know what?" Rush had tears in his eyes and desperation in his voice.

"Oh, baby," I whispered.

"Simon!" Snow shouted frantically. I saw Rush's father's hand raise at the same time I heard the gun go off.

The sheer force of the bullet sent me crashing into Rush. It was like my chest was on fire, and I knew I'd been shot, but nothing else was making sense. All I could think was, *Where is Rush?* I jerked my head from side to side searching to see if Rush was harmed, and I watched his face crumble as if he were breaking apart. What was happening?

"Are you okay?" My voice sounded funny.

"Simon." He slid out from under me and rolled me on my back, and I felt him pressing on my chest with so much force, I wondered if he was ripping my heart out. "Help him!" Rush yelled, tears running down his beautiful face.

"Don't cry, Rush." But when I tried to lift my hand to touch him, I couldn't. "What's happening?"

A loud crash made me jump, and Rush toppled against me. I heard him whisper in my ear as the world around us fell apart.

"I wanted to get a chance to love you."

And then there was nothing.

CHAPTER TWENTY-NINE

Rush

There was so much blood, and I couldn't stop it. "Simon, open your eyes, goddamn it!" I didn't know what was going on around me. There were shouts, and it felt like a bomb went off in the house. I was only concerned about saving Simon from dying.

"Rushmore!" My father shrieked, but I couldn't find it in me to care. He'd shot Simon. Why would he do that?

My hands were crimson as I pressed any and every fabric I could find on the wound; then a pair of pale clean hands joined mine. I was surprised to see Fred there.

"Let me look."

"What?" Why would I do that?

"I'm pre-med, Rush. I know more than you, now let me look." I'd had no idea he was pre-med at all. I knew nothing about Fred. But what choice did I have? Moving my hands, I watched as Fred, the man who had made my life a living hell for three years, tried to save Simon's life.

"Seems like the bullet went through his back and out the front, that could be good, but…" Fred was talking to himself or maybe to me, I didn't know and didn't ask.

"Rush." Someone called my name in an eerily calm voice. "Rush, look at me." But I had to watch Simon, protect him if Fred tried anything. "Sweet boy, I need you to see me." I knew it was Snow.

"I can't, I have to watch over him, he…I told him I would. I need to…he has to live."

"I will fucking kill you!" The thunderous voice shook me to my core, and I did look away from Simon in time to see Christopher Manos storm over to my father, grab him by the shirt with one hand and punch him in the face with the other, over and over again.

"No," I whispered. "Please, no more." I covered my head and curled to the floor next to Simon.

"Rush." Snow was practically covering me.

"We gotta get him to a hospital now," Fred shouted.

"Christopher!" Snow yelled.

Christopher dropped my father and came over, his obsidian eyes flickering over to me and then to Simon. This was the man the press wrote stories about in front of me. The mobster who put up a closed sign on his emotions and did what needed to get done.

"Follow us, Rush," he said, scooping Simon up in his arms.

Seeing Simon leaving, I was able to jerk myself out of my fear bubble and move. I glanced at my father, whose face was bloody, but he was awake and glaring at me.

"He stays here. I'll return for him." Christopher spoke to Mace, who nodded.

"Rushmore, please," my father pleaded but I couldn't…I followed Christopher out of the house and to the car.

He got in, still holding Simon and even though he was a

grown man, Christopher held him like he was a fragile baby. I was next to him, and Snow was in the passenger seat while Frank drove to the hospital.

I couldn't make out what Christopher was saying to Simon, but I wasn't meant to; they were words for him. Maybe he was praying. Did mobsters pray?

Simon wasn't moving, and I placed my hand on his leg since it was the only thing I could touch. I rested my cheek on his knee and silently prayed. I asked my mom to please help him. She may have wanted to end her life and not be there to love me anymore, but she wanted the best for me, and Simon was just that.

"We're here." The car came to a screeching halt and then it was chaos. Nurses, doctors, Snow doing his best to explain what happened through sobs. And then silence.

Simon was taken through the double doors, and none of us could follow. I stood in the hallway beside Christopher and Snow as we watched our world get wheeled away.

I walked around the waiting room in a numb sort of trance for hours. I watched the sun go down through the large windows. The news was reporting something about a burglary but nothing about Simon. I went back to pacing.

"Drink this." A cup of coffee was thrust in front of me.

"I'm not—"

"Drink it." I noticed the person who handed it to me had dried blood on their hand and I followed the arm to the face. Fred.

"Why are you here?" I wasn't being rude, I just didn't understand.

"I've been here the whole time. Snow told me to come since I was helping Simon."

"Simon…" I turned toward the double doors, but there was no doctor there.

"Still in surgery, Rush. Please drink the coffee before you collapse."

I went to hold the mug, but my hands were shaking too much to grip it, so Fred helped me drink. He encouraged me to sit down and once I did, I realized how much my body hurt.

"I never meant for any of this to happen," Fred said.

"I don't understand why you were with my father."

Fred grimaced at the mention of my father. "He was charming, Rush. I know you can't see that about him. He filled this place in my life left empty by my own father and treated me with so much care. At one point there wasn't anything I wouldn't do for him. But it wasn't real for him."

"What does that mean, 'wasn't real'? I keep feeling like I'm missing something."

"I don't know the whole story, but your dad, shit, Rush." Fred sniffled, and I realized he was crying.

"What, Fred?"

"He's a monster."

The waiting room doors opened, and I turned, thinking it was the doctor, but it was Christopher, the guy who threatened me, Bic, and a redheaded man in a suit.

"Shit," I heard Fred say. "That's my dad."

Liam Brennan and Christopher Manos together in this hospital? I was tired of the violence. All I wanted was Simon smiling at me and kissing me.

"Rush." Christopher sat beside me while Liam went next to Fred. "Simon is out of surgery but in critical condition. I don't know many details, but as of right now he's alive." His voice was so monotone, I couldn't gauge an emotion from him.

"Can we see him?"

"Not right now. We need to speak with you, Rush." Christopher rested a hand on my shoulder.

"Uhm, okay."

"There's a private room one of the nurses said we could use; let's go there so no one can overhear us."

I wasn't going to argue with Christopher or anyone who was acting as lethal as he was.

"You too, Fred." Liam stood and began to walk out. Fred, Christopher, and I followed him to another room where he closed the door behind us. Bic was instructed to stand outside and make sure we weren't interrupted.

"Rush, what I'm about to tell you is going to be hard to hear but nevertheless, you need to know, because there's a lot your father needs to answer for." Christopher guided me over to a chair, and I sat down.

"Frank called Simon from Liam's house to let him know what was uncovered. None of it did we expect, but it's real."

"I have proof and can show you whatever you'll need to see to prove what you're about to hear." Liam scowled when he talked, as if he'd never learned how to smile.

"Okay."

Christopher took a deep breath and if I didn't know better, I'd have thought he was worried. "Your mother, she died by suicide, that's what you were told?"

"Yeah. She suffered from depression most of her life. She killed herself and my father found her."

Christopher nodded. "It's not true."

"What part?"

"All of it," Liam answered. "Allow me to explain. See, your father came to me three days before your mother died to purchase a delicate gun. He wanted it to be silver with flowers, really nice for his wife." Liam shrugged. "Many people come to me for things, so what did I care? I got it for him, he paid. Then I see the news of your mother's death and set up a meeting with your father."

My father bought my mom the gun that she'd killed herself with?

"I thought for sure he'd deny any part in her death, but he didn't. Right there, in the middle of my office, he said he killed her. When I asked why he would do that with a gun I'd supplied him with, he said she wanted to get you away from him, to let you be a dancer or whatever the fuck you wanted to be. But see, your father needed you to be an Abernathy because"—Liam chuckled—"this is the fucked-up part."

It felt like someone was wrapping barbed wire around my heart, and waves of nausea crashed over me as I listened to them tell me this story.

"Your father gets five million dollars a year from the university for working there, and your grandfather made sure an Abernathy always would be there, or they'd lose their income, and the board would take over. Only way to get your father out of the university's hair was either for him to die, which they weren't gonna do, an Abernathy refused to be employed there, or he broke the rules."

"I don't get it. If Rush graduated and worked at the university, wouldn't his dad stop getting the money and Rush would start?" Fred asked.

"He would, if his father ever told his son that, which I'm guessing he didn't and was intending to pocket it all for himself," Christopher answered.

"And with me graduating next year and working there, my father would continue to get the money."

Liam nodded. "Thing was, the university has been making my life a living hell. They've been trying to buy properties to expand, on your father's orders, and I'd had enough." Liam sighed and glanced at his son. "I don't like that Fred is gay, and I found out your father was fucking my kid. Did some digging and found out that was against the university's rules. So I reported it to the board with a little proof."

"And he got suspended." Fred's brows were furrowed.

"I know you need time to absorb all this, Rush, and when we're done you can." Christopher patted my hand.

"Your father knew who Fred's father was and was recording every encounter with Fred. We think his intention was to blackmail Liam at a later date in exchange for help should he need it again like when he bought the gun and killed your mom." Christopher took out a USB flash drive and slid it over to Fred. "Frank found the recordings on this drive."

Fred fisted the drive, anger rippling through him, easy to see.

"There were other drives, Rush."

I looked at Christopher. "Wh…what was on them?"

"We only started going through them, but your father was trying to buy out a shit-ton of properties and drive Liam out of town, either that or make Liam have to come to your father for help, and between owning all the properties, and having the recordings of him and Fred, he thought he'd have a mobster on his payroll."

"What about Holly?" It was a stupid question, I couldn't understand all I was hearing.

"Holly? The secretary?"

"Yeah."

"She was a real secretary, but your father was there only to help with events and the rest of the time he spent his days—"

"Wreaking havoc on everyone's life like a narcissistic sociopath," I answered as if on autopilot.

"I'm so sorry, Rush," Christopher said. But I didn't want to hear it. I wanted to see my father and hear him admit it.

I stood abruptly and moved toward the door. "I want to see my father."

"Rush, you can't, he has to—"

"Please, Christopher. I deserve to hear it from him!"

I closed my eyes, knowing if I were told no, there would be nothing I could do about it.

"Okay."

CHAPTER THIRTY

Rush

My body was tired, my head ached, and my heart was shattered. I wanted to feel a rage burning inside me burst through and tell Christopher none of that about my father could be true, that he was a loving and kind man. But he wasn't. And as I sat in the car on my way to see that man, I wracked my brain, trying to find one moment in my life where he'd hugged me and supported me. One time he'd said he loved me.

Then I thought about my mother. While she and my father hadn't shown affection, she always had a hug and smile for me. She would sit in the garden and watch me act out my favorite musicals or sit with me in the music room and listen to me play on the piano. Cheering when it was over.

She was depressed a lot. I remembered more times than I could count where she would be in bed for a whole day, cry a lot, and drink. So when I was told she killed herself, I'd rationalized it in my head. I'd been so angry with her for years because she'd left me, but she hadn't. She was taken from me instead.

"I want to warn you, Rush. Your father isn't here on vacation. I ordered my men to tie him to a chair; it won't be pretty." I didn't say anything and when Christopher got out of the car, I followed.

"Christopher?"

He stopped by the front door. "I have another question before we go in. I don't know why I need to know it, though."

"Go ahead and ask."

"Why did Liam try and kill Simon and me, then? If he was mad at my father, what did the two of us have to do with that?"

Christopher smirked. "I asked Liam that too. He hates Abernathys, and when he saw you with Simon Manos in his territory, knowing what all your father was doing, and on top of it the snooping we were doing on the Brennans, it pinged his radar, he assumed there was some huge takeover coming, and he tried to stop it."

I couldn't imagine someone like Christopher Manos accepting that answer. "And that's it? He's off the hook because of an oops?"

The side of Christopher's mouth quirked up. "I never said that, Rush, I just don't attack two wolf packs if I can take them out one at a time instead."

Made sense, I guessed. I just didn't want to be here when Christopher went head-to-head with Liam to collect his pound of flesh.

I followed Christopher inside, noticing how the place had been cleaned up and the window in the living room was boarded up. I could only assume that had something to do with the loud explosion I'd heard. Someone had mentioned how Bill had crashed through a window—that had to be it. We were walking through the living room when I froze. The stain where Simon lay bleeding hours before was still there. So much blood, he should have died. My father had been aiming to kill him.

"This way, Rush."

I followed Christopher toward a closed door. He didn't hesitate and when I entered the room I saw what he was talking about.

My father's arms were tied to the armrests of the chair. Each leg was tied as well, and he had duct tape over his mouth. His eyes widened when he saw me, but I quickly looked away.

Bill was at one end of the room and Mace the other.

"How's Simon?" Mace asked.

Christopher filled them in, and I just kept playing the questions I wanted to ask my father on a loop in my head. When I couldn't take it anymore, I went over to him.

"You killed Mom," I said. Christopher and the others stopped talking. My father couldn't respond because his mouth was taped. "You tried to kill Simon. The only two people in this whole world who ever cared about me. And for what? Money, power, property?"

He mumbled, trying desperately to say something to me, more lies, I was sure. "And all this time, all these years I wanted to be an entertainer, and you guilted me into getting an English degree to hold a respectable position at Abernathy so you could collect the five million dollars a year that would be mine."

I shook my head and leaned closer, looking into his swollen eyes. "You do events for the university, and yet you thought my getting a theater degree or something in the arts was beneath our name?"

He glared at me, the anger in his soul all that was left in this man.

"Maybe you never loved me at all. Maybe I was just another pawn in your game to take over the world, I don't know. But I can't save you. I don't know how, and I'm not sure you're worth saving." I chuckled. "Mom always said to me, 'Everyone is worth saving.' Funny how she would believe in you, and you never believed in her."

I stood up and walked over to the window. It was dark out, no sun, no view. And I realized I didn't need his answers.

"There was a time I would have done anything you ever asked of me because I thought it was the way to get you to love me. Now I realize I never stood a chance." I turned to look at him, and there was still so much anger. "I don't know what Christopher and Liam have planned for you, but I'll mourn you just the same. If you're lucky and you get to live, know that you're dead to me. I never want to see you again."

With nothing left to say, I walked out of the room at a fast pace, went to the bedroom that I shared with Simon, collapsed onto the bed, and cried. I sobbed into his pillow for everyone gone, hurt, or fooled by the person who should have protected and loved me unconditionally. I cried until there were no more tears left, only sleep.

THREE WEEKS LATER

"I can't eat any more Jell-O." Simon pushed it away. "I want a burger with bacon, and onions, holy shit, I really want that."

I laughed and rolled the tray away from his bed. His recovery had been long. It was touch and go for the first week, and then he stabilized. This was the first week he was in a room outside of the ICU.

"I promise as soon as we get out of here I'll buy you a triple-decker bacon burger."

"Don't play with my heart, Rush. It's been bruised." He pointed to the large bandage across his chest. He'd forever have a scar where they'd had to crack open his chest, and I'd kiss it for as long as I was in his life. It was a reminder of how fragile life was and how I'd almost lost him.

"I'm not teasing. I will."

He tapped his lips, and I leaned down to drop a kiss on them.

"Do you want me to read to you, watch a movie, or see what's on the news?"

He shrugged. "I'm sure Snow and them will be by soon, so let's watch the news and later, when they leave, we can do something else."

The hospital had us in a large suite and one of the nurses brought a bed in for me to stay with him, for which I was grateful. But I had a feeling it was one of the Manoses that had made it all happen.

We'd been watching the news for fifteen minutes when a picture of my father came on the screen. Simon raised the volume.

"I don't have a lot of details, Jim, but I'm being told by the police chief that it appears to be a suicide. Now this family isn't a stranger to suicide about—" Simon shut off the TV, but I just stared at the blank screen.

I'd known he was dead; in my heart I'd known. But I'd assumed I'd never hear about it.

"I'm sorry, Rush." Simon reached over and squeezed my hand.

"No, it's fine, really. I…it's fine." I felt like an orphan…How strange at my age to have that feeling.

"Let's watch that movie. If anyone comes by we can tell them to piss off."

I mustered a smile for Simon, but I needed to move, to walk. "I'm sure I'm going to get slammed with questions from the university and police, and I think before that happens I want to pretend my life hasn't been a total lie."

"Rush, it hasn't."

"Simon, come on, it has. Will you be okay for a little bit? I need to go somewhere, but I promise to be back soon."

He cocked his head, and I could tell he wanted to argue with me, but he acquiesced. I gave him a kiss and left his hospital room to do what I needed to so I could move on with my life. My real life.

CHAPTER THIRTY-ONE

Simon

Rush was gone for two days. He called and let me know he was fine and that he'd see me soon. Penelope had heard I was in the hospital and visited me. It was no secret who I was anymore, and she completely understood why I'd never told her. When she left I had a feeling I'd never see her again, but she seemed happy and in love with her new boyfriend, so I was happy for her. Snow and Pops hadn't really left my side, and every time I got antsy about Rush, Snow would tell me I had to let him make his own path.

"But what if he's lonely and needs help?"

"Eight, I'm sure there are moments he is very lonely and times he needs help, but it's up to him to ask for it and for him to come to you. He will. Believe me, I know what Rush is feeling. Mothers and fathers are our life no matter how old we get. I know what it feels like to be betrayed by a parent and to lose the one who was your biggest ally."

I don't know how I'd missed the similarities between Snow's and Rush's lives. "Shit, Snow. I'm sorry."

He waved me off. "Hush. My life is great. Sure, I could stand to stop having heart attacks because you or Christopher almost die, but other than that it's filled with love and people who make me want for nothing."

"I want Rush to have that, to feel loved and have a family that wants nothing more from him than he's willing to give."

"He will, Eight, I promise."

It was day three when Rush came back. He looked tired but okay. He walked straight over to my bed and kissed me long and hard.

"I missed you," he said.

"I've literally been where you left me."

He chuckled. "Thank you for letting me go and not stopping me. I had to do what needed to be done."

"Am I allowed to ask you what you did?"

He smiled and sat in the chair beside the bed. "First, I went to the cemetery to talk to my mom. Apologized to her for being angry at her all these years. And before you tell me she would understand, this was my catharsis journey, not yours."

I held both hands up. "I said nothing."

"Mmhmm. So, then I went to the university and dropped out."

"You did what?"

"I can't stay there. I met with the board and made a deal, I asked for one year's income for me to leave. They were all too happy to give it to me. They won't have an Abernathy underfoot anymore, and I'm five million dollars richer."

"But where are you going?"

He held up a finger. "I'm getting there. I then went to your room and packed up all your things. I called Christopher and he took them. I also asked him not to say anything to you about it."

"Am I dropping out too?" I smiled because where Rush went, I followed.

"Yeah, we can't stay here, you know that. You're not meant for this place."

"Okay…"

"I made arrangements for my father to be cremated and his ashes scattered over the Garden of Statues at the university. It's the place he lived and died for, so he should stay there."

"Anything else you did?"

"I had dinner with Fred at The Falsetto Café. His father is still pretending he doesn't exist, but he's okay. He's coming to terms with everything that happened, and he says each day it's easier. Then I talked Luis while I was there. He was thrilled I was getting away from all this, and while he was sad to see me go, he made me promise to visit. Which I will absolutely do."

"Rush?"

"Yes, Simon?"

"Can I ask where we're going now?"

He laughed. "Home. Your home. We can complete school near Haven Hart, and you can be with your family."

"You're my family."

"I love hearing that, and I'm totally in the market for a new one. But with them is where you belong."

I reached out, glad when he took my hand. "You belong with us too." He didn't argue but he didn't agree. "Let me prove it to you."

"Oh, I intend to let you do that because I have nowhere else to go."

"With me you'll always have a place. Now climb up here and lie with me."

He removed his shoes and slid in beside me. He couldn't rest on my chest, but just having him close meant everything to me.

"What about that winter charity auction you were going to do?"

He sighed. "Yeah, I'm sad I'll miss that. I called Em and

explained everything and with my father dying, they understood. I'm sure the one-million-dollar donation I made helped too."

Laughing, I lightly tapped his shoulder. "I'm sure that was a balm on his burning heart."

"It was the least I could do."

"So, what you're saying is that you don't have five million dollars, you only have a meager four million?"

"I know, however will you love me?"

"I already do love you, Rush."

He lifted his head and gifted me with a radiant smile. "I love you too, Simon."

"Phew."

He laughed, and for the next little while it was just Rush and me, alone but not lonely. Never lonely again.

―――――

A week after Rush returned, I was discharged from the hospital. I wanted to go home to Haven Hart and eat a fucking burger, but the doctors had requested I stay in town for a few more days before traveling. So, there I was, in a hotel with Rush, Snow, and Christopher.

"You can both start classes in the new year. Here's the course list." Christopher handed papers to each of us.

"Wait, where is this we're going?" Rush asked as he read the courses.

"Since you're living at the house, I figured going to Hart University made sense." Christopher shrugged and didn't even have the nerve to look a little embarrassed over his apparent interference in our futures.

"Don't we have to apply?" Rush chuckled as he circled a few classes he found interesting.

"Silly, sweet boy." Snow winked at Rush. "Just pick your classes."

I could only shrug when Rush looked at me wide-eyed. "What classes are you going to take?"

He rolled his eyes and handed me his paper. He'd circled only arts classes, and I knew he was going to be massively successful.

"Forging your path," I said to him, feeling a nudge on my foot from Snow.

"Yeah, I think it's about time."

Taking Rush's face in my hands, I pulled him to me and kissed his lips. Lips I planned on kissing for a long time.

"It's definitely time for you to start living your life."

EPILOGUE

Rush

Christopher Manos's house…mansion…was insane. I knew I'd get lost at least ten times and need a search and rescue team to find me. But it wasn't just the size of the place, it was the people…and the dogs.

When we walked through the door, this elderly woman ran up to Simon and hugged him until he shouted that he needed to breathe. Simon introduced us; her name was Maggie, and I found myself getting the air squeezed out of me.

Then I met Frank's wife, Lisa, followed by the rest of the household. I knew it would take me a long time to remember the names and faces of this place. Then there were the dogs, or Germadoodles, as Snow called them.

They were huge and liked to jump. We spent a good ten minutes letting the dogs greet us before going upstairs to Simon's room.

"I'm sorry," he apologized once he'd closed his bedroom door.

"For what?"

"The assault."

I laughed as I placed my suitcase on the bed. "Are you kidding? That was wonderful. Don't take it for granted."

He smiled softly and wrapped me in his arms. "I never will."

THREE MONTHS LATER

"How were your classes?" Simon asked as he walked with me back to the car.

"Good, we have to write a play and direct it. I'd rather perform, but it's all important. I should know this stuff too."

"Oh, a play! Do you know what you're going to do?" He clicked on the fob and I got into the passenger side of his new Mercedes.

"I was thinking of making it a Mafia love story."

Simon started the car and faced me. "Oh, really? And who are the main characters?"

"I was thinking a lowly guy who is living a modest life, minding his own business, and some dangerous sexy man comes crashing into his life and turns his world upside down. There's a car-chase scene I'm trying to figure out how to stage. And of course, casting the dangerous mob boss."

"Mmhmm. What does this mob boss look like?"

I shrugged playing it off like nothing. "Dark hair, tall, broad, gorgeous skin, onyx-colored eyes…oh, you know, like Christopher."

That earned me a slap on the arm. "Very fucking funny."

I laughed all the way out of the campus and onto the main road toward home.

As the town of Haven Hart passed us by, I realized how at peace I felt. I couldn't remember a time in my life where I'd been this content. And it was strange that I'd found that in the mansion of a mob boss.

Sure, it was still dangerous, and I knew there were operations going on that I wasn't privy to. I'd heard Bill and Christopher talking in the kitchen the other morning about when they would be dealing with Liam Brennan. They hadn't stopped talking when I came in, and in that moment, I knew I was completely trusted.

I appreciated everything the Manos family was doing for me and while Christopher wanted me not to worry about money, I quickly explained that I had enough to get by. He went on about being proud I took the university for what I was worth and patted me on the shoulder.

"My pops needs me to go to a meeting tonight, it's about Liam. So, I'll be late for movie night."

"Okay."

"Did you want to come to the meeting?"

"Why?"

"He tried to kill you too, Rush. You have a say."

I was quiet for a few minutes until I saw the large black gate with the two Ms on it.

"I will always have your back, Simon. I will defend your family to the death, hand to God. But it's not my life by choice, it's yours. This is who you are, and I love you and accept that. I trust you're doing what it is you have to and need to in order to keep me and the rest of your family safe."

"But?"

"But I spent over twenty years living a life my father wanted for me. I'm doing what I want for the first time ever. I want to enjoy it." I reached out and placed my hand on his leg. "If you need me, though, I'll always come."

Once his car was parked, he shut it off and faced me. "I always need you, but I want you to live your own life. I just wanted you to know I have no more secrets from you and will always keep you in the loop."

Smiling, I kissed him for a moment before pulling back. "No more Secret Simon?"

"Never with you ever again."

"Then that's all I need."

OTHER BOOKS BY DAVIDSON KING
HAVEN HART SERIES:

Snow Falling

Hug It Out

A Dangerous Dance

Snow Storm

From These Ashes

Triple Threat

Raven's Hart

Haven Hart Novels

Secret Simon

Joker's Sin Series

My Whole World

To Die For

Heart Beats

Taste Of Fear

Collaboration with JM Dabney

The Hunt

Standalones

New Tricks (Book 10: Ace's Wild multi-author series)

Sticky Fingers

CLOSING NOTE

Thank you for reading Secret Simon. I hope you loved these guys as much as I did. Please feel free to leave a review I'd appreciate it and if you want to find some free short stories and exclusive material join my Facebook reader's group: https://www.facebook.com/groups/DavidsonKingsCourt/

Also, keep up with my new releases and info on book, translations, audios, and more by joining my newsletter: https://www.davidsonking.com/subscribe

ACKNOWLEDGMENTS

Secret Simon was a book I didn't realize I'd write until the epilogue in Raven's Hart. I knew it wouldn't follow that story arc, but it was part of that world, nonetheless. I thank all my readers for that. They fell in love with Eight and wanted to see the man he'd become, and I hope you're not disappointed. Thank you for loving this world so much.

Thanks to my husband and children for letting me do what I love so much and encouraging me to keep on keeping on even when I feel like giving up.

To my mom, you're the loudest cheerleader I have and without you always pushing me, I'm not sure I'd be where I am today.

Hugs and love to all the people who made this book shine: Flat Earth Editing and Proofreading, Hope and Jess, you make cleaning up a book fun and a learning experience. To Anita Ford for getting the book at its rawest form and at it's cleanest. You're outstanding. To Jenn Gibson, who always gives me amazing emotional feedback that betters my work. Morningstar Ashley, you make the prettiest covers for my imagination, and Luna David, you make this inside glorious.

Thank you to my friends: Annabella Michaels and Jaclyn Quinn for listening to me vent when I want to rip my hair out. You're awesome!

ABOUT THE AUTHOR

Davidson King always had a hope that someday her daydreams would become real-life stories. As a child, you would often find her in her own world, thinking up the most insane situations. It may have taken her awhile, but she made her dream come true with her first published work, Snow Falling.

She managed to wrangle herself a husband who matched her crazy and they hatched three wonderful children.

If you were to ask her what gave her the courage to finally publish, she'd tell you it was her amazing family and friends. Support is vital in all things and when you're afraid of your dreams, it will be your cheering section that will lift you up.

Check out my Linktree for all links: https://linktr.ee/davidsonkingauthor

Made in the USA
Middletown, DE
09 October 2024